'Plato has furnished for all posterity the pattern of a new art form, the novel, viewed as the Aesopian fable raised to its highest power.'

Friedrich Nietzsche
The Birth of Tragedy (1871)

THE MUSIC OF TIME

Twenty-Four Fables for Today

PHILIP ALLOTT

Copyright © 2022 Philip James Allott

Front-cover image
N. Poussin, Danse sur la musique du temps (1634-36).
© Wallace Collection, London, UK / Bridgeman Images.

The moral right of the author has been asserted.

Apart from any fair dealing for the purposes of research or private study, or criticism or review, as permitted under the Copyright, Designs and Patents Act 1988, this publication may only be reproduced, stored or transmitted, in any form or by any means, with the prior permission in writing of the publishers, or in the case of reprographic reproduction in accordance with the terms of licences issued by the Copyright Licensing Agency. Enquiries concerning reproduction outside those terms should be sent to the publishers.

This is a work of fiction. Names, characters, businesses, places, events and incidents are either the products of the author's imagination or used in a fictitious manner. Any resemblance to actual persons, living or dead, or actual events is purely coincidental.

Matador
Unit E2 Airfield Business Park,
Harrison Road, Market Harborough,
Leicestershire. LE16 7UL
Tel: 0116 2792299
Email: books@troubador.co.uk
Web: www.troubador.co.uk/matador
Twitter: @matadorbooks

ISBN 978 1803132 228

British Library Cataloguing in Publication Data.
A catalogue record for this book is available from the British Library.

Printed and bound in Great Britain by 4edge Limited
Typeset in 14pt Minion Pro by Troubador Publishing Ltd, Leicester, UK

Matador is an imprint of Troubador Publishing Ltd

This book is dedicated to my parents who selflessly devoted their lives to their children.

The author acknowledges his debt to Aesop, Plato, Theophrastus, Plutarch, Boccaccio, Chaucer, La Fontaine, La Bruyère, Perrault, Shaftesbury, Landor, and George Eliot, and their Fables and Dialogues and Characters and Lives and Tales and Characteristics and Imaginary Conversations and Impressions.

Front-cover image.
DANCE TO THE MUSIC OF TIME
The four figures dancing in
a perpetual circle may represent
Poverty, Labour, Riches, and *Pleasure*.
Apollo or, let us say, *God* is overhead in his chariot. *Time* is playing the lyre.

Stories nos. seven, twelve and nineteen are versions of chapters in the novel *Eusophia* by the present author.

CONTENTS

ONE. THE SPOOK'S TALE   1
Carré on Charming.
Changing the world intimately.

TWO. THE ARISTOCRAT'S TALE   19
The Way of the World.
Losing the past.

THREE. THE YOUNG ITALIAN'S TALE   33
Gotham and Gomorrah.
Sudden aging in Manhattan.

FOUR. THE SPECIAL WOMAN'S TALE   47
People like us.
A defiant woman of the people.

FIVE. THE THINKING BUSINESSMAN'S TALE   61
Alma Mater-Pater.
Marketing ideas that could change the world.

SIX. THE INTELLECTUAL'S TALE   75
Hampstead Heights.
Metanoia in north London.

SEVEN. THE AMBITIOUS YOUNG MAN'S TALE　91
A chancer gets a chance.
Beginning to become himself.

EIGHT. THE HOLY WOMEN'S TALE　105
Virtue Rewarded.
A convent decamps.

NINE. THE PHILOSOPHER'S TALE　119
Mind Games.
Too much information about philosophy.

TEN. THE IMMORTALS' TALE　135
Pandora's Other Box.
Time past is time present.

ELEVEN. THE FRENCH WOMAN'S TALE　149
A France More Profound.
Love at last in Quercy.

TWELVE. THE HOLY MAN'S TALE　163
Re-thinking in tranquillity.
Between the past and eternity.

THIRTEEN. THE ENGLISH MEN'S TALE　181
A well-ordered life.
Talking as a way of being.

FOURTEEN. THE DIPLOMATS' TALE　197
UNCLE 12
Rebellion in the diplomatic ranks.

FIFTEEN. THE CONVICT'S TALE　215
Crime and punishment.
The injustice of justice.

SIXTEEN. THE ANXIOUS THINKER'S TALE 231
When ignorance is bliss.
'Tis still necessary to be wise.

SEVENTEEN. THE BANKER'S TALE 247
Missing person.
Self-doubting.

EIGHTEEN. THE CONNOISSEURS' TALE 263
The mystery of art solved.
The last of the few.

NINETEEN. THE RICH YOUNG MAN'S TALE 281
An accidental hero.
In the right place at the right time.

TWENTY. THE ALIEN'S TALE 295
This England.
Dystopian utopia.

TWENTY-ONE. THE HUMAN BEINGS' TALE 317
A species facing extinction.
Homo neque sapiens.

TWENTY-TWO. THE TECH WIZARD'S TALE 335
Rescuing humanity from itself.
A revolution in the mind.

TWENTY-THREE. THE GARDENER'S TALE 355
Cultivate your garden.
The simple life. if all else fails.

TWENTY-FOUR. LOST TIME REGAINED 373
The future of the past.
Brave world that has such people in it.

EPILOGUE 391

THE CHARACTERS

Most of them are also present in no. 24.

Adam Hutton, English connoisseur.	18
Bill Sykes, convict.	15
Cardinal Castelfranco, priest.	12
David Barclay, rich young man.	19
Denis Dobson, businessman.	5
Don Quixote, ingenious gentleman.	11
Dorothea Dorn, young Austrian historian.	12
Edgar Sibling, young English man.	7
Eliza Glampworthy, aristocratic cook.	2
Ernie Wilde, English man.	13
Frank Price, English man.	13
Gavin Meredith, scientist-engineer.	22
Gertrude Stein, writer.	10
Greta May, German connoisseur.	18
Harry French, spy.	1
Jack Gaddi, American in England.	21
Joe Giorgione, young Italian man.	3

John Doe, banker.	17
John Singer Bunyan, philosopher.	9
Maggie Blyth, defiant woman.	4
Manu Narayan, wise man.	20
Marie-Hélène Biron, French woman.	11
Matthew Broad, historian.	20
Mollie Maine, gardener.	23
Septimus Blenkinsop, solicitor.	2
Serena Stangle, intellectual.	6
Sister Monica, nun.	8
Steve Ruskin, people-watcher.	16
Thomas Grange, aristocrat.	2
William Fortescue, butler.	2
UNCLE (participants anonymous).	14
Various revenants.	11

One

THE SPOOK'S TALE

CARRÉ ON CHARMING
Changing the world intimately

Harry French had hardly been in Berlin for ten minutes before he got himself into trouble. He sang the Horst Wessel Lied on an U-Bahn train for no good reason. He didn't sing it either enthusiastically or sarcastically. He may have remembered it from a previous posting in Berlin. It may be the only German song he knew.

Admittedly, he had had a schnapps or two too many at the PJ Club, which was my fault. Admittedly, he had been in Ulan Bator twenty-four hours previously. He was justifiably tired. But he should have known better.

The train wasn't crowded, but, as it slowed down at Uhland Strasse station, a tall thin man with a pale face and staring eyes came towards us, stabbed Harry in the shoulder with a short-bladed knife without saying a word, got off the train and disappeared.

Another passenger was an off-duty policeman. As we were waiting for the ambulance to arrive, he took down Harry's details in his notebook. Harry didn't claim diplomatic impunity, but he was economical with the details. It didn't help that his passport was chock-full of visa stamps from many countries, some of them rather exotic. The paramedics dealt with Harry's wound in the ambulance. The stabbing seems to have been essentially symbolic. Harry was free to sleep the sleep of the incorrigible.

He was to be my assistant in the trade and industry side of the work of the Embassy. Selling high quality British goods and services in competition with high quality German goods and services is not easy. Tiptree preserves, Scotch whisky, haggis and popular musicians sell themselves. Haggis had acquired something of the prestige of caviar in Germany, being an acquired taste and very expensive. Otherwise, it was all rather difficult.

Harry's reputation had preceded him. I was anxious. His personal file said that he was very much his own man, but also a good team-player, a combination for which there must surely be a German word ending in *keit* or *lich* or both. It turned out to be true.

Diplomacy involves great numbers of lunches and dinners and cocktail parties. Someone said that cocktails are to diplomacy what incense is to the Roman Church. A means of grace through prayer. Cocktail parties are certainly good places to meet people who then invite you to their parties to meet other people and so on, until you soon know everyone who matters in the country in question.

Harry was in his element in such a process. It was his job to know as many people as possible. He spoke French and German and useful amounts of various other languages, some of them learned on the pillow perhaps, as people say. In that field of human endeavour, he had the advantage of being able to function *à tous azimuts*, if you get my Freudian drift. He could learn a great deal about rich and powerful people and newly poor and infamous people.

For example. An American colleague in Berlin had introduced him to a wealthy American politician whose rigorous Evangelical façade concealed a less than noble private life. He was much involved in imposing tariffs on the import of European goods, including Stilton cheese and haggis and English sparkling wine. Harry visited him at his house in Georgetown and they became friends.

It was at the time when Donald Trump was on his imaginary throne in Washington DC for the first time. Needless to say, Trump rejected his political ally's advice, which he saw as too favourable to the British. But Harry had made a friend in a very high place in America. Soft power works in mysterious ways, even among allies. It had a lot of work to do when the United States hesitated to join in the two World Wars while it contemplated the interesting possibility that Germany might destroy the British Empire.

It had always been a rather special relationship, since the US invaded Canada in 1813 and Britain had to invade Washington and destroy the White House and the Library of Congress, and then again when Britain hesitated about its neutrality in the American Civil War which nearly destroyed the United States. People of Harry's kind play an important part on both sides of such a very special relationship, as they had throughout British history.

Then there was the time when, quite by chance at a party in Berlin, Harry had met the wife of a well-known master of some capitalist universe. Harry was especially proud that he didn't bat an eyelid when she inadvertently referred to a rather obscure Greek gentleman who was with her as her husband. *Mein Mann.* She apologised for the slip of the tongue in the most convincing way.

Some straightforward research, straightforward when you already half-know the answer, allowed Harry to confirm that they had been married, morganatically as it were, and presumably bigamously, if she was already legally married to her master of a universe. She and the Greek gentleman had married in a Greek Orthodox church on a Greek island that I will not identify here and which Harry took the trouble to visit, knowing that she and her official husband often visited the island on their yacht.

Next time he met her, he said that he had visited the beautiful Greek island in question. Thereafter she was all-charm towards Harry, not her normal manner, and Harry had another friend for life in a very high place, and another source of other less permanent friends in high places.

Harry's work may seem rather old-fashioned in a world in which electronic means allow governments to spy on every word and thought and deed of their own citizens, seeking out internal enemies, and everyone else and everything else everywhere. Electronic magic has weaponised the replacing of wax seals, the steaming open of envelopes, the intercepting of telephone calls, and the placing of microphones here and there. It means that governments are flooded with more information that they can usefully use about the doings of their own people and the doings of foreign governments, including supposedly friendly foreign governments.

Governments have always spied on their own citizens. Governments have always used fake news and fake confessions extracted by torture. The spymaster of King James I of England got people to believe that Guy Fawkes had somehow managed to secrete thirty barrels of gunpowder into the cellars of parliament, months before the annual opening of a parliamentary session.

Harry French's work is in a different, but also hallowed, tradition at the soft power end of the diplomatic spectrum. His job is to recruit agents of influence who may use their political and economic power in ways favourable to the British national interest. He is seeking out potential friends, not potential enemies. His employers know that there may even be occasions when a friend may feel obliged to prefer British interests to the interests of their own country.

The reader will surely want to know if Harry himself was vulnerable to such seduction in the service of the public interest of some country other than his beloved Britain. He never said much about what he was doing in Ulan Bator immediately before he arrived in Berlin. Without any difficulty, I confirmed that he had not been posted there, nor did he have any visible connection with the British embassy there. Visiting Mongolia is surely not on the agenda of even the most sophisticated traveller.

What I did know, and he didn't conceal it, is that he had acquired some useful knowledge of Chinese. Heaven knows how. No one could conceivably learn Chinese by pillow talk. But it meant that, at diplomatic parties, he was able to throw in some convincing bits of Chinese, when speaking to Chinese diplomats and visitors from China. Did his superiors in London know that he had acquired this extracurricular skill? If they knew, did they know how he had acquired it?

This led me to wonder whether they would think of him as a particularly useful asset or else as a security risk. Could he possibly be a double agent of influence? But, not being one to sow doubt about a close colleague who had become a close friend, I followed a British tradition by not pursuing that particular line of enquiry any further.

Harry's mental crisis came out of the blue. A complete surprise. However, I believe that it is in the public interest that I should speak about his mid-career crisis. I mean public interest in the strict sense, not merely the interest of an insatiable scandal-loving public.

I had come to know him as a rock-solid, cold-eyed, perfectly balanced observer of the human condition, including all the meretricious glamour and glitz, and the seedy layer below the surface of even the most sophisticated human society. The *peccadilli*, and indeed the *peccati*, of the rich and powerful could be pathetic and revolting or amusing and interesting. He would readily admit that he himself enjoyed the glamour and the glitz.

He had already told me that recently, after some twelve years in the spooking business, he had concluded that the experience he had been accumulating, in all the places where he had been posted and elsewhere, contained an important truth about the human condition. Of course, countless other people had experienced such a revelation at some time during their careers. But, for Harry, it was not a general suspicion or a cynical judgment. It was a matter of fact. He was a man of facts.

So now he made a special appointment to see me, saying that he had something very important to tell me. I assumed that it would be something he had discovered that might rock the pillars of German society or German politics.

'We've all been wrong,' he said, 'all the time, about everything. The Book of Genesis. Copernicus. Einstein.'

That was not what I expected to hear.

'The human mind is the centre of the universe.'

'*Eppur si muove.*'

'The universe is nowhere. It moves at the speed of the human imagination.'

I decided to accompany Harry in his frenzy.

'*$U=mc^2$, where U is the universe, C is the human mind, and M is the motive force of the human mind.*'

He ignored my brilliant suggestion.

'There was nowhere for us to fall from, or to. The human world is flat. If you walk around the human world, the edge is always in front of you, you never each it.'

I must admit that, at this point, I began to feel a twinge of anxiety about this exceptionally level-headed colleague and friend of mine. Flat-Earthing is a sure sign of mental weakness.

'All social philosophy, all the story of human history treats the human world as vertical. Who dominates whom? For Lenin the only question to ask about the constitution of a society is: Who whom? That is wrong.'

I ventured to say that at least Lenin knew what he was talking about.

'No. He was wrong. The right question is: who conspires with whom?'

In the best Foreign Office tradition, I was already drafting in my mind a message to his superiors in London, wondering how much of the gory detail I would include, to explain Harry's mental collapse.

'The human world is horizontal. A horizontal network of conspiracies, and conspiracies of conspiracies. Political, economic, religious, intellectual. And they are all struggling to have the biggest effect in society. And you, the citizen, can come and go, free to join whichever conspiracy looks promising at any time. That is the true meaning of legally protected freedom.'

Suddenly, I experienced a doubt. Had Harry got a point? His experience of the real world was second to none. And he was, in principle, as intelligent as anyone I have known. Some rapid redrafting, also in the Foreign Office tradition, tacking into the wind.

I ventured to suggest a hint of understanding.

'From my life-time in the business of so-called diplomacy,' I said, 'I think you may be right that we do spend an awful lot of time in seeking alliances and compromises that only we really know about and understand, but which can affect the lives of millions of people.'

'And you do that in a closed conspiracy with politicians, and in another closed conspiracy with the biggest economic interests. Secretly, telling each other that they are doing all this in the higher common interest, as if there were a higher common interest somewhere other than in your own imaginations.'

'And we rely on the intellectuals to give our imaginings some aura of sanctity.'

'And they are conspirators in proclaiming the sanctity of their ideas.'

Scrap the draft message to his superiors in London, who are probably already very well-aware that they are themselves a conspiracy.

'What I can't see, Harry, is how we could continue to function in our customary ways if we accepted your rather novel view of the world.'

'We could and should function much better, much more effectively, much more truthfully, much more benignly.'

'I tell you what, Harry. Let's go and have a glass or two of German wine and plan our own little conspiracy.'

We went to the Embassy's local pub in the Adlon Hotel. A happy hunting-ground for Harry. A waiter winked at him. We were soon in a philosophically creative mood.

'It seems to me, Harry,' I said, 'that your conspiracy theory of conspiracies could also include benign conspiracies, doing good things.'

'That's the whole point. A horizontal view of the human world includes good conspiracies naturally, alongside all the power-seeking and money-seeking and evil-doing conspiracies. The true constitution of every society does much more than distribute power among the holders of public power. It starts with families.'

'And families are in principle a little local conspiracy,' I said, 'and capable of doing good, or so we always hope.'

'And schools and universities and museums and football clubs and churches, and charities and pressure-groups. Benign conspiracies, in principle at least.'

For a while we stared into our glasses, savouring the possibility of a better view of the world while consuming the Adlon's version of tapas. I broke the silence.

'We who work in diplomacy deal with a human world of one hundred and ninety-two conspiracies called states, few of which, if any of which, one would dream of calling benign.

'I spend a good deal of my time archeologising people's lives,' Harry said, 'digging thorough the shiny surface to discover what lies beneath. And I do it, supposedly, in the national interest. States are not human.'

'But states are human frailty written very, very large.'

'Couldn't we imagine a horizontal conspiracy of all horizontal conspiracies?' Harry said, speaking slowly, choosing his words. 'We could call it *Humanity*. A human conspiracy serving the best interests of all human beings.'

'That would be pushing things a bit. A human race capable of acting benignly for the benefit of the human race? I suppose we can imagine it, Harry, after a few glasses of German wine. We can certainly imagine it, Harry. You say it's our imagination that makes the universe, so it must be us who make the human race what it is, or what it could be.'

Harry and I were probably now thinking the same strictly personal thought. My diplomating and his spooking could be made more interesting, more exciting even, more useful even.

'God bless and preserve the human imagination,' Harry said prayerfully.

'Amen. God bless Humanity. Let us pray that we two at least may carry on diplomating and spooking with our minds and hearts newly enlightened.'

'And, who knows, we might be able to spread enlightenment like gold dust across the seedy worlds of power and politics, national and international.'

'Apostles usually end up as martyrs, Harry.'

'Saints in the service of Humanity.'

'Martyrdom in the service of the Crown.'

Time for a modest, unexpectedly cheerful, dinner.

MORAL
They also think who serve their country.
Beware!

* * *

We have not blown the cover of Harry French (if that is his real name) by writing about him here. Other security services know who people like him are and what they are doing. There are other people doing other work about whom that may not be true.

Two

THE ARISTOCRAT'S TALE

THE WAY OF THE WORLD
Losing the past

'Will you be staying for lunch, Master Thomas?'

'Is Mrs Glampworthy still doing the cooking, Fortescue?'

'Yes, sir. She is.'

'Last time I was here, her soufflé failed to souffle properly for some reason.'

'Soufflé is not her strong suit, I think.'

'Does she have a strong suit? As a cook, I think she's rather no-trumps. But I suppose I should see the solicitor.'

'He will be lunching, sir. He was a devoted friend of his lordship, your late uncle. God rest his soul.'

'A surprising number of his devoted clients seem to have been dying recently. And his prosperity seems to increase by leaps and bounds.'

'His clients have expressed their gratitude most generously, sir.'

'I don't doubt it. I keep forgetting his name, Fortescue.'

'Septimus Maximus Blenkinsop.'

'Quite a moniker for a country solicitor. Large family, presumably.'

'Only child, sir. Your uncle told me.'

'Maybe there were six others, born too soon, if you know what I mean. Of smaller stature.'

'Maybe.'

'So Mrs Glampworthy is still a fixture?'

'His lordship rescued her in her time of need. They became close.'

'Time of need, Fortescue! She had married an Episcopalian bishop in Las Vegas.'

'The Glampworthies were a Mayflower family, apparently. The bishop regretted it immediately. So Mrs Glampworthy told me.'

'Did Mrs Glampworthy regret it?'

'She regretted the straight-up Bourbon whiskey. Never touched it again.'

'Not really suitable for a delicate English rose like Lady Eliza Tolpuddle.'

'Of the Shropshire Tolpuddles, sir. A much older family then any Mayflower family. But it seems that a Mayflower name is useful in American high society.'

'The Americans are as snobbish as the rest of us, Fortescue. No class-system. My foot. My uncle told me that the first Glampworthy got to America by mistake. He was escaping from a father with a wronged daughter and a blunderbuss. He hopped on a boat going to Holland. He didn't know that the next stop was America. after they'd picked up some Puritan refugees.'

'Must have been a bit of a shock.'

'Must have been. It was the social media that did for the bishop and Ms Glampworthy in the end.'

'Why are they called social media, sir? They don't seem very sociable.'

'They're an electronic lynch-mob, Fortescue. Judge and jury and executioner. No right of appeal. No stay of execution.'

'Lady Eliza took refuge in Shropshire. And his lordship, your late uncle, rescued her and brought her here. The Episcopalian bishop became a Cistercian monk, I believe.'

'The wages of sin are mostly embarrassment, Fortescue. So that was a bit excessive.'

'Her ladyship, your late aunt…'

'Not late, Fortescue! Aunt Amelia Jane is living it up in Portofino with smarmy Italian aristocrats who kiss her hand and call her countess. What they lack in liquid cash, they make up for in houses and work of art.'

'I'm sorry, sir. My tongue slipped. Your aunt comes home every year for the shooting in August. She's very handy with a gun. Could come in useful vis-à-vis the mafia.'

'I don't think there are mafia in Portofino, Fortescue.'

'Your uncle's father often went there. He backed the wrong side in the Wallis Simpson business, didn't he, and had to make himself scarce.'

'Yes. He thought the Prince of Wales was a bounder, out and out. He was sent to Coventry in his London clubs, until it all blew over. Things usually blow over in the end, don't they, Fortescue?'

'It's the way of the world, sir.'

'Aunt Amelia Jane could go south, and become a mafia *capo,* or would it be *capa*? A lot of liquid cash. In brown envelopes. So, this Maximus Septimus chap…'

'Septimus Maximus, sir.'

'Whatever. This bloke Blenkinsop. Loyal

family legal adviser and friend of the wealthy. What's he up to now?'

'He's just bought Holme Farm.'

'The Archers' place?'

'Yes.'

'What does he mean to do with it?'

'He has planning permission to turn it into a health spa and wedding venue, with an alpaca farm. Or it may be ostrich. I forget which.'

'It had better be alpaca. They're quiet. Ostrich make an awful noise, booming and hissing. What do the villagers think?'

'They're daggers drawn. Some of them feel a personal need for a health spa. Some of them think it's vandalism. There are meetings and placards and shouting in the pub.'

'A bit of civil war is a good thing for a village, Fortescue. Helps to relieve the awful boredom of living in the country. If Blenkinsop is coming for lunch I could ask him about my uncle's will, couldn't I? Any idea what my late lamented uncle will have done? He was a living embodiment of the unpredictable, in a good sort of way, of course.'

'He will have been well advised by Mr Blenkinsop.'

'You think! Holme Farm is next door to our place!'

'The solicitor helped your uncle to get a proper survey of his estate, which should be helpful in the probate of his will.'

'Worth millions, we've always assumed.'

'I heard your uncle say that he was rather surprised and disappointed by the value the surveyors put on it. Not that your uncle would ever have thought of selling it. It's been in your family for centuries.'

'Without a mortgage in sight, as far as I know.'

'Not having children, your uncle and your aunt were always the best of friends, despite everything. I'm sure he will have done the right thing for her.'

'Despite everything. There was a lot of everything to be in despite of, on both sides, Fortescue. At least you can say that my aunt's dreadful Italian hangers-on would be at home here, helping to turn our prized family possessions into liquid assets.'

'I've never trusted Italians, sir.'

'Their Renaissance made us civilised, Fortescue, or as civilised as the English are capable of being.'

'I hope they have learned something from us, sir.'

'That remains an open question. Speaking of

the … the solicitor! I hear a car approaching. A Lamborghini XL. Unmistakeable.'

'It's a very red car.'

'Spot on. Tell him I will receive him in the gun room.'

'You know all the guns are under lock and key, sir.'

'I don't plan to shoot him, Fortescue. Not yet, anyway.'

'Good to see you again, Mr Blenkinsop. I've heard so much about you. How are things with you?'

'I can't complain.'

'I don't doubt it. Can you tell me anything about my late uncle's will?'

'May I offer my condolences on your loss? He was a fine gentleman. I was always close to him, as I was with his father.'

'I don't doubt it.'

'Your uncle has given a generous life-time annuity to his wife. She will be able to live comfortably.'

'I wouldn't be so sure of that.'

'Your brother has inherited his uncle's title.'

'I can't see him leaving his job at the Mowbray Melton investment bank in New York, to entomb himself in the English countryside.'

'The estate will continue to be looked after by the excellent Estate Manager your uncle relied on so much. He is married to my niece Jocasta.'

'He's not called Oedipus, by any chance?'

'No. Ralph. I can vouch for his excellence myself.'

'I don't doubt it. Do I get anything?'

'Your uncle has left you his collection of toy soldiers, his fishing-rods, and a legacy of £100,000.'

'That's nice of him.'

'The legacy will be delayed for two years. And there is a condition. You must undertake to take care of your aunt Amelia Jane for her remaining days.'

'She certainly doesn't need any looking after by me. Is it possible to challenge such an absurd condition?'

'Anything can be challenged, but I would have to advise you that the legal costs would certainly exceed the amount of your legacy.'

'I don't doubt you would. Can one challenge the whole will for bribery and corruption?'

'As I say, you can challenge anything. But that would be a novel sort of claim. I would have to advise you that the case would certainly go to the Supreme Court with two Q.C.'s on either side at all levels. That would not be cheap.'

'I wouldn't think of doubting your advice. And who would decide whether I was observing the condition on my legacy?'

'The trustees.'

'And you are a trustee, I imagine.'

'And your brother and Mrs Glampworthy. Your uncle has left her a very generous legacy.'

'I suppose I could always say that a soufflé that doesn't souffle is a masterpiece of *nouvelle cuisine*. Make peace with her.'

'Excuse me…?'

'Do you feel like a traitor to your class, Mr Blenkinsop?'

'What class do you have in mind, Mr Grange?'

'The class of those who, down the centuries, have held the hand of great landowners, warts and all, through ups and downs and thick and thin, wealth and poverty, crime and punishment, sanity and madness. And did not expect much more in the way of a reward than a roof over their heads and regular meals, knowing that the whole shooting-match ultimately depended on their loyalty.'

'Times change.'

'*Chi sta bene non si muove.* Countless people depended on the survival of the whole shooting-match. Doing their best.'

'I have always done my best for all my clients.'

'I don't doubt it.'

After lunch, I asked Fortescue what he had made of it all.

'I have family in New Zealand, sir. And Mrs Glampworthy has her family in Shropshire. We are dispensable. We are the past. The future has no need of us.'

'But you and I are both English, Fortescue. And the English have never simply accepted the inevitable. Ten centuries of history show that. Kings have had to learn that. Foreign countries have been mystified by our crazy persistence.'

'Things do get better, sir. My father and grandfather were miners in Yorkshire. A hot bath once a week in a metal tub in front of the kitchen fire. My grandmother was a parlour maid in the house of Earl Fitzwilliam. She died of tuberculosis. Two of my grandfather's brothers died in France at the Somme. They were boys really. I have worked in some good houses, none better than your late uncle's. I think I've always been fair to those who have served under me. I've had a good life.'

'You're right, of course, Fortescue. I have always been a younger son, with no great expectations, bound to make my own way. My gallery in London has been a success, depending on the whims and the money of people who will always be much richer than me.'

'It's the way of the world, sir. That's what my Sunday-school teacher used to say. You've got to make the best of what you're given.'

'But then the turning world takes the shape of someone like Septimus Maximus Blenkinsop.'

'And that's not easy to put up with, sir.'

'It's not easy, Fortescue.'

'There's something else our Sunday-school teacher taught us. I've never forgotten it. It's sort of a prayer.'

'Share it with me now, in our joint time of need.'

'We are all masters. We are all servants. We are ruled by other people, and by the natural world that gave us life. We rule other people, and the natural world that gives us life. May we be the best of servants and the best of masters, in all that we do.'

'Amen, dear William. Amen. We'll have to learn how to live for the future.'

'Amen, Thomas. Amen.'

MORAL
The future is at the mercy of the present.
Beware!

* * *

Three

THE YOUNG ITALIAN'S TALE

GOTHAM AND GOMORRAH
Sudden aging in Manhattan

Everyone eventually lands up in Manhattan, like moths unable to resist very bright lights. All are migrants. Some flourish and stay. Some burn up, and return defeated to the hopelessness of some small town far distant from any bright lights. Some hang on, living from day to day. Some end up in the East River, by their own hand.

Some acquire duplex apartments with views over Central Park. Some live in two rooms in the West Village, writing poetry and a novel that will never begin to see its end. Some take to crime, shoot and get shot. Some take to Wall Street, and quickly learn the rules of the game of making the kind of money that quickly comes and can quickly go.

Some tire of the heat and the cold and the

rain and the snow. They migrate to the bright lights on the other coast which are remarkably similar lights, with the same frenzy and impermanence, but with the addition of never-ending sunshine and beaches. Some of them eventually come to pine for the bright lights of Manhattan, which comes to seem improbably homely and humane, at least as seen across a few thousand miles of nothingness in-between.

Joe Giorgione was the exception that proves several rules. He was not in New York as a migrant or by his own choice. He was the son of a member of a permanent mission to the United Nations. He was an outsider inside. He simply fell in love with the city, its squalor and its glamour.

When his parents were posted to Geneva, Joe remained and became a locally based employee of the permanent mission. Manhattan, with its temptations and its possibilities, lay at his young and relatively well-heeled feet.

Do not suppose, dear reader, that his parents simply abandoned Joe to the temptations and the possibilities of New York City. He would be living with Alison, a senior British member of the UN colony, in her apartment on East 51st Street. It would be a sort of gap year before he took up a place at a British university. It would be useful to learn a little more about the folkways of the North American tribes.

Joe was an unusually serious, not to say solemn, person for his age. He was familiar with the concert halls and opera houses and theatres of New York. He was an habitué of the wonderful New York Public Library. He spent time searching for genius in the smallest galleries of the Village. He was a member of an Italian literary society.

He went to church religiously every Sunday at St Patrick's Cathedral. He made regular donations to the super-elegant St Bartholomew's Church, for its work in giving a temporary home and food to the homeless.

It may not have been necessary, after all, for his parents to alert friendly members of the UN colony to keep an eye on their over-sensible son.

Bill, a young member of the Australian permanent mission to the UN, helped him to move his stuff to his new lodging. Then they had a cool pint of Guinness in an Irish pub on Third Avenue, and a burger *du jour* with fries at a Greek diner on Second Avenue. They bought some fruit from an all-night Vietnamese grocery store. They sat on a bench, breathing the familiar smell of air-conditioner exhaust fumes from a Chinese laundry.

At much the same time, far across town, at much the same latitude on the island of Manhattan, the Russian mafia were holding a meeting in a room behind a Russian restaurant. The meeting was terminated ahead of schedule by a bomb that destroyed the restaurant and the room behind the restaurant.

We only know this because it was in all the newspapers on the following day. The New York Daily News had an editorial comment saying that tax dollars should not be wasted on trying to identify the perpetrators because (a) the true perpetrators would never be identified, and (b) the perpetrators would do the same thing again, when necessary.

It is not only the United Nations that shows us that the nations of the world can live together, if not in peace and harmony, then at least in all kinds of pragmatic co-existence in every-day life. The good order of the mafia world is an eloquent model for international relations.

Joe slept soundly in his new home after a busy day, wakened only occasionally by the sound of the sirens of fire-engines and police cars from the fire station and the police precinct in East 52nd Street. We owe so much to the skill and courage of those who risk their lives to save us from ourselves.

A first night at the Metropolitan Opera is intimidating, especially for someone who has struggled to tie his black bow tie, and someone who could not decide if her evening gown was too long or too short. Joe and Chloe, from the UN Secretariat, were intimidated.

They were using very expensive tickets left behind by Joe's parents. Mercifully, the opera was not Wagner. Less mercifully, it was a new opera by an American avant-garde composer who was a good deal too *avant* for most of the audience. But American audiences are generous. The barrage of applause at least equalled the barrage of coughing.

To see the highest levels of New York society together in one place is an impressive sight. An implosion of wealth and power. Improbably, it reminded Joe of a time in the south of France when he had seen a herd of pink flamingos, tall and proud and self-absorbed. Or a very high High Mass in St Peter's Basilica in Rome. The highest levels of the Roman Church displayed their various costumes, affirming layers of hierarchy. Each was more powerful than the layer below, from the Pope downwards.

That was a link with the quasi-religious rituals at the Metropolitan Opera. The rich and powerful are acutely conscious that not everyone is of equal power and wealth. In the human world there is always someone else to whom you are inferior. There are castes within castes in a society which has a race-system and imagines that it doesn't have a class-system. Were there more than ten people of colour in the most expensive seats? Some would say that even that would be progress. America moving-on.

The rich and powerful are not deceived by their own glitz and glamour. They leave the mythologising to lesser mortals. They are performance artists performing their place in society as rich and powerful men and women, stars in their own right on that night in that place, no further effort required. The men indistinguishable from each other in their black-tie or tailcoats. The women asserting the couple's superiority in subtle codes of dress and jewellery.

Joe and Chloe walked back across town in the darkness. The avenues were still full of the noise of traffic. The side-streets were mostly deserted. The myriad traffic signals went on issuing their orders to cross or not to cross the street, but there was hardly anyone there to obey. New York City at night is another place, a different dream, a better dream, a calmer dream.

But we all want to know the answer to the question: did Joe Giorgione's year on his own in New York lead him to succumb to its temptations, or was he content to exploit its possibilities?

It's not an easy question to answer. To begin with a conclusion. At the end of the year, Joe was several years older, and a different person.

His Australian friend Bill introduced him to nightclubs, straight and gay and mixed. Joe began with the gaze of an observer, overwhelmed by watching the bizarre behaviour of attractive young people whose barely clothed and sweating bodies moved endlessly in mechanical response to the meaningless rhythm of music. But then his gaze changed into a gaze into himself, as he found himself feeling at home, at home with the kind of things that must have been hidden in his unconscious mind, out of harm's way.

The young people seemed to have gone beyond pleasure into a sort of existential despair, knowing that their temporary relationships would always end, and always means always, in their being hurt and betrayed. Joe had not known before that he was capable of feeling existential despair. He had to admit now that there was a lot about himself that he had not known, and which he must have successfully repressed or sublimated.

There were Sundays now when he could not go to church, having become too aware of sin and evil. Not the conceptual Original Sin of the Book of Genesis, but the infinite variety of evil manufactured by actual human beings, evils any of which he now knew that he himself could probably commit given the right circumstances, evils which religion seemed unable to prevent in its mission of human self-transforming.

Joe attended sophisticated dinner-parties, catered, because New Yorkers do not do cooking. Like all southern Europeans, he loved conversation for its own sake, a life-enhancing exchange of ideas and feelings. But these were not life-enhancing conversations. It is not that the guests did not have ideas and feelings. New Yorkers have ideas and feelings about everything. But there was no sense of a conversation as anything other than something that people use to accompany fine food and fine wine. He had come face to face with existential despair in social relationships.

He attended concerts and plays and exhibitions, but he seemed to have lost the joy that he had found in wondering at the creations of the amazing power of the human imagination. Watching their audiences now, it seemed to him that such things were failing to engage their humanity, let alone to enhance it, other than as things that intelligent people should witness as part of a conventional good life, a good life that they didn't really think of as particularly good.

He called it his Pirandello moment. We are the author, the actor, and the audience of the play that is our life. And we're not much good at any of those things.

He attended meetings of the General Assembly and Security Council of the United Nations, speak-easy on the East River. Speaking for the huddled masses of the world, who were hardly aware of their existence, the privileged representatives of governments spoke easily and endlessly about their respective crimes and misdemeanours, and yet the world never changed.

A second conclusion about Joe's year of freedom is: if you can't become a mature human being in New York, you won't become a mature human being anywhere. Joe Giorgione had matured, not like wine in oak casks in a cellar, but like a fragile tree that finds a way to flourish in whatever the sun and the rain and the winds throw at it.

The painful paradox was that all this meant that it was hard to find anyone with whom to share his discovery, since the people he met were all paid-up members of what he was now seeing as a human race in a poor state of health.

Then he met a girl called Jane. It was like in a fairy-story. She seemed detached from a world of which she was, to all appearances, a normal member. He called her his White Swan, as in *Swan Lake*. She called him Joe the Joke, because of his seriousness.

She had the joy of life, or what he could now call existential hope. The diametrical opposite of Tolstoy's Katyusha, she seemed to have a smile in her soul, surely the most delightful human characteristic. She was not religious in an institutional sense. She believed in the redemptive power of smiling and laughing. Joe soon felt able to return to church again, remembering that a religion might also proclaim existential hope, and that the poor long-suffering faithful can do their best to aim at it as an ideal.

Jane had come to New York when her parents sold their farm in Maine. They had decided to urbanise themselves in later life, as an experiment, an experiment that has continued. Jane's maturity was of that rare kind that comes from a perfectly good relationship with her parents, whose own maturity probably came from their being the latest in generations of farmers. Farmers are like trees with deep roots, in the matter of maturity. She had come to share in the maturity of her parents, which was surely the original purpose of family life, even if that may be hard to believe in the modern world.

Jane had taken a degree in psychology at New York University, and a further degree in psychiatry. She now worked in child psychiatry. Joe had not been able to restrain himself from saying that there was something to be said for a sane psychiatrist.

They were happy when they were together, which is saying a lot about two people. It was too soon to talk of marriage. University in England might undo the good work that the best and the worst of New York had done for Joe. But who knows? If there were two people on the beleaguered planet Earth who were apostles of existential hope, maybe there could be a million. And then the Earth might become a little less beleaguered.

'Thank you, New York. Thank you, Jane.'

'For what?'

'From sadder and wiser to brighter and better in one move, in the great Mah-jong game of human life.'

Jane laughed.

Joe smiled.

MORAL
*Existential hope is the other side
of the coin of existential despair.*

* * *

Four

THE SPECIAL WOMAN'S TALE

PEOPLE LIKE US
A defiant woman of the people

'I'm writing my autobiography.'
'Don't be silly, Maggie. You can't.
'Why not? I've got a word-processor and ink-jet stuff and paper.'
'People like us don't write autobiographies.'
'We do have lives, don't we, like everyone else.'
'Not like everyone else. You've got to have drawing-rooms and weekends in the country and Romantic goings-on in Venice and people called Hugo and Lavinia and winters in the Caribbean and rosy-cheeked children with fair hair.'
'You watch too much television, Jane. Anyway, your Bill and what's-her-name went to Barbados.'
'For the cricket.'
'And they went to Venice. They've got the nodding gondola to prove it.'

'You've got to have books and paintings and servants and antique cars and hunting and shooting and fishing,'

'My late husband fished, most of the time,' Maggie said. 'When he was out-of-work. Like the Queen Mother.'

'In a reservoir, Maggie, not the Highlands of Scotland. And the Queen Mother wasn't trying to get away from her husband, like your Bob was trying to get away from you.'

'You've always taken his side, Jane.'

'He was my brother. For all his faults.'

'We've all had our ups and downs. God knows. A lot of downs. Like everyone else.'

'You've got to have wild romances with tall handsome men that end in tears, or worse, and officers in the Guards who disgrace themselves, and uncles who are vicars, and do peculiar offences and pay the price.'

'You read too much Jackie Collins, Jane. That's not the real world, you know. My grandad's dad couldn't read or write. He was a private in the Duke of Wellington's Regiment, serving king and country. He was gassed at Ypres, which the soldiers called Wipers. He died ten years later, never having got back his health.'

'Death is the only certainty in life, Maggie,'

'But unnecessary death isn't. It's a crime.'

'Your grandad was a POW, wasn't he, Maggie,?'

'Yes. He was in the Green Howards. He was one of the last out of Dunkirk and went straight off to Singapore, serving king and country. Prisoners of the Japs had a story to tell. They never told it. Unemployed for years, he read poetry and did watercolours. He read a lot. He knew everything about the American Civil War.'

'There were many people like that, Maggie.'

'Naming no names, Jane, you had a cousin who did his time for an interesting thing involving cars, and the export thereof to the Middle East.'

'He got into bad company, Maggie, as you know very well. And he got himself into the middle-class, sort of. Middle-class people can write autobiographies, even if they didn't fish with the Queen Mother in Scotland.'

'Yes, but they have a first chapter about their awful childhood in a run-down semi in Liverpool or Brixton, outside toilet, parents who abused them, physically and mentally, and so on. And all the rest is about how clever they've been in doing well for themselves, in films or television or football or business, or whatever, with big houses in Kensington or Cheshire.'

'So not quite people like us.'

'We've done well for ourselves, Jane, people like us. All things considered. And our children should do even better, shouldn't they?'

'But we're still where we started from, Maggie. And who could want to read about that?'

'It's the story of ninety-nine percent of the human race, Jane. Why wouldn't people want to read about that?'

'So that's why you want to write about you. You've got an axe to grind.'

'I've got something to prove, Jane.'

'About nobodies who stayed where they were?'

'Nobody is a nobody. We all become somebody. And we haven't stayed where we were. People like us have moved on a thousand miles compared with what our parents and grandparents were before the two wars.

'The autobiography of a nobody who became a somebody while they stayed where they were.'

'No, Jane. The autobiography of a human being like all other human beings who remained human, despite everything.'

Maggie Tate had got it all planned-out in a file on her computer.

She had a title, which she would willingly change, if she thought of something better.

A Yorkshire Woman from Sheffield. Not like any other.

She didn't want it to be chronological. Parents, birth, schools, jobs, marriage, children, middle age, loss of her husband, the life of a widow. No. She wanted it to have the style of a BBC documentary. *Thematic.* Human progress comes in many different forms. Hers is a story of one kind of human progress.

An overriding theme was that she knows she is much more intelligent and a much better person than the jobs she had had. How could that have happened? The same must be true of countless other people like her. But Maggie Blyth is rather like the 'great ladies' of Victorian Britain, totally self-confident in themselves, clear-eyed about the deeply unsatisfactory society into which they had been born. And she is not a duchess or a countess.

An important theme for Maggie is *heredity*. People like her know little about their ancestors, but there must be something of them in us. She was one of those lucky people who can say that they had good parents who made a good home.

She had Irish people in her background. Some of them went to America to avoid dying from hunger in the Famine, when the English treated the Catholic peasants as sub-human. Worth further research. She must have some of that defiance in her, surely. Not to mention a bit of a gift of the gab, and a touch of the blarney stone.

So far as *education* is concerned, she knew that she had left school desperately uneducated. She got on well in her two schools. She got good reports. She had some good teachers, doing their best in difficult circumstances. Maggie was unusual in being able to sit quietly reading a book on her own, like her grandfather.

'People pay pots of money to private schools that give only one thing to the wretched kids,' she said. 'Self-confidence. I've always been self-confident. I would have made a good teacher. Teaching is sharing. I'm a sharing person.'

She knew, what many of her fellow pupils also say, that the education she received at school didn't prepare her to make a better life. It simply evaporated when they left school.

She had read a great deal ever since, and she chooses serious programmes on the radio and TV, which allow her husband to escape to his garden shed, to his fishing, and the pub, where he could meet his men friends away from the women in their lives, their own Garrick Club.

So far as *religion and morality* were concerned, she has a strong sense of duty, and of right and wrong. She must have acquired it osmotically from her parents, good people who made a good home, so far as they could, and from her grandfather, a victim of his service to king and country. She was very fond of him, and he had been very fond of her.

'Osmotically,' she told Jane, 'means catching something without noticing that you're catching it.'

'Like the flu or herpes,' Jane said.

'More or less.'

Maggie was not religious. She had been baptised in church, and married in church, and she sent her Bob to his rest with a church service. She knew some Catholics, who had pangs of guilt if they missed Mass on Sunday, and who had a sort of aura around them, as if they were in touch with something higher. But, like most people she knew, she didn't find religion necessary in her life.

So far as *sex* was concerned, she and people like her were not obsessed with the thing. as the middle and upper classes seemed to be, and it drives them mad. Sex was for making children.

Of course, there were children born before marriage and outside marriage. And people had flings when they were on holiday in Spain. And they were well-informed about the feckless goings-on of celebrities. That was just the way of the world. It made a good topic of lively conversation in the workplace canteens, their Garrick Club for men and women.

So far as *employment* was concerned, she has had very many jobs, none of them worthy of her intelligence or her personality. She had only once been unemployed. Never again. She was humiliated by having to sign in at the Labour Exchange. She hated the very words *dole* and *benefits*. Never again.

She admired the men who sweated to their death, inches away from the flames of the blazing furnaces in the steelworks, and the miners who coughed their way to their death, doing backbreaking and dangerous work miles underground, their skin permanently ingrained with coal dust. Her mother's family had been a mining family, in the villages to the east of Sheffield.

She admired the 'little mesters' who made cutlery and tools and swords by hand at home, with great skill and aesthetic sense. Her grandfather had been one of them. She envied plumbers and carpenters and electricians and painters, who had great skills, and their own dignity to match. She had no skills.

'For a good life, people should get apprenticed to a decent trade. And then they're also useful to the country. Everyone should have further education for the rest of their lives, not just people who go to university. So they can become the people they know they could be. It's criminal that almost everyone dies without becoming what they could be.'

'But even we are useful to the country, aren't we?' Jane said.

'Yes. The country depends on millions of ordinary people doing ordinary jobs without which the whole thing would come to a halt. All the others with their money and their privileges depend on us doing our work. I can't see why nobody ever mentions that. Why aren't we respected as much as bankers and businessmen, who couldn't exist without us?'

Maggie had worked in many different jobs requiring no special skills. The high point was when she worked at Coles and Walshs, before she had children, and then when they first went to school. She only had to moderate her Sheffield accent a little. Like all Yorkshire accents, it conveys a feeling of warmth. But 'madam' now, not 'love'.

They were the shops patronised by the Sheffield middle classes, living in houses with gardens, close to the dramatic Derbyshire countryside, western suburbs on the city's tree-filled seven hills. They were protected by the west wind from the dirty air and foul smells and the noise of the east end of the city, with its desolate slums and polluted watercourses.

She and Jane lived in-between, in Crookes and Walkley, and counted it among their blessings. Jane's father had been a Labour city councillor for The Moor, ironical name for one of the city's most deprived wards. He was chairman of the Transport Committee in a city proud of its public transport.

The Industrial Revolution had turned a country town into a bustling city of great wealth, unequally distributed, with all the wonders and the horrors of industrialism as a social phenomenon.

Maggie's *politics*, and the politics of people like her, are realistic. She is proud to be English and British. She is a strong monarchist, on sentimental grounds, but also on practical grounds. She distrusts politicians instinctively, people who didn't know what it means to spend your whole life trying to make ends meet, week after week, month after month.

She, and people like her, vote in elections. Around the kitchen table, they dissect what the politicians said they would do and would not do. They make their judgment, and they vote accordingly.

She refuses to call herself working-class. She calls herself, and people like her, ordinary people. Most people in the world are ordinary people.

She knows that there are millions of people around the world who are ordinary people living a bad kind of life. Exploited, oppressed, enslaved, with no life-choices of their own to make. She knows that ordinary people in countries like hers, especially young people, are being corrupted by the social media and by debased politics, and by the degenerate ways of living of the supposed role models known as celebrities.

But the future is too important to be left to natural causes. Good people must speak out. They must help to make a better future for everyone. The unstoppable power of great numbers and overwhelming fellow-feeling.

Maggie will put all these things into her book. She knows what the last sentence will be. *Human beings should be self-respecting and respected by other human beings.* A better philosophy of the good life.

Maggie tried to get Jane, her sister-in-law, to agree with her. But, for Jane, Maggie Blyth was not someone quite like her. She read too much, thought too much. And she had a gift of the gab and a touch of the blarney.

'In your heart of hearts,' Maggie said, 'you know I'm right.'

'In my heart of hearts, the best thing in life is a lovely glass of cool draught Guinness, with a lovely cheese sandwich.'

Maggie knew that Jane was joking. And Jane knew that Maggie knew.

They both smiled. The smile of the best sort of human friendship.

MORAL
Not all people like us are people like us.
We're all unique

* * *

Five

THE THINKING BUSINESSMAN'S TALE

ALMA MATER-PATER
Marketing ideas that could change the world

'I've solved a problem that no human mind has ever solved before. It will change the world.'

'Well done, Dobson. I always knew that you had it in you. Can you share it with me, as we Americans say?'

'Nay, as we Yorkshiremen say,'

'I thought you were Scottish.'

'Binational and bilingual. And there never were two greater nations.'

'What about the ancient Greeks or the Mormons, although, as we applied humanists say, they did have the advantage of a *tabula rasa* or blank sheet. Could you at least tell me what the problem you have solved is, even if you can't tell me the solution?'

'Nay. I cannae. You might claim to have a genius-moment or a light-bulb moment, and you would put in on Facebook, and I would be ruined. I've got to get intellectual property priority. As an academic, you must know that.'

'Can I make some guesses about the insoluble problem that you've solved, and you could nod or shake your head if I am getting close?'

'Guess all you like. My lips are sealed.'

'How did people manage before someone invented zero? What is the square-root of the square-root of minus one? Why didn't someone buy Proust a new Remington typewriter? Would the Reformation not have happened if Luther had known about Imodium? What happened to the siblings of Jesus Christ? How many children did the first Popes have? If Venice is sinking, where is sinking to? What about the fifty-seven people who had a better claim to the British throne than William of Orange? If Byron was the first modern man, who was the first modern woman? Do monkeys see a monkey in the moon? Am I getting close?'

'You're like all academics. You know everything and you know nothing. You, with your Harvard alma mater.'

'Alma pater.'

'No such thing.'

'When I say the words *alma pater,* the words *alma mater* immediately enter people's minds. Then I've done my daily duty of gender equality effortlessly, as it were.'

'Who was Alma anyway?'

'Not the colourful Alma Mahler, I promise you. The word means *soul*.'

'And Harvard has a soul?'

'A richly endowed soul.'

'Do you never take anything seriously?'

'Irony is to wisdom what wine is to the French. It improves the digestion. You could put your discovery into a novella like Voltaire. With your Dr Pangloss as a hero, not a figure of fun.'

'I'll need your advice in applying for a research grant of one million dollars or pounds, to complete my work and make it functionable.'

'You would have to reveal everything in the grant application.'

'That's out then.'

'You could try crowd-funding. Then you could be obscure as you like about your discovery, so long as you say it would end world poverty and deal with climate-change.'

'And that wouldn't be untrue, Gatsby. You have been like a friend to me, Gatsby, since we first met in North Borneo. I think I need you now as a sort of alma pater.'

'I'd be glad. And an alma mater too.'

'When people like Copernicus or Newton or Darwin suddenly found the truth, what did they do about it?'

'Certainly Copernicus and Newton and Darwin worried about losing what you call their intellectual property priority. They knew that many other people had been thinking much the same thing for a long time. So they became very secretive and defensive about their great idea. What they did was to get other people to call them geniuses who had solved a problem that no one else had ever solved. Kepler did it for Copernicus. Voltaire did it for Newton. Huxley did it for Darwin. Call it good Public Relations if you like. Presentation is everything.'

'That's exactly it, Gatsby. That's why I need you.'

'But you, Denis, wealthy investment consultant, surely know enough about Public Relations to know that the moment you enter the world of Public Relations, Truth, with a capital T, flies out the window, like a bird that was trapped and couldn't find its way out.'

'But what I would be selling is The Truth, like never before.'

'Excellent, Denis. You're selling THE TRUTH. You've got to make people believe it. This vacuum cleaner re-invents the idea of the vacuum cleaner. This book re-writes the history of France. This novel puts Proust in the shade. This footballer is the GOAT. This politician makes all other politicians seem like minnows. Whatever minnows are.'

'So you yourself wouldn't need to know much about my new solution to all the problems of the world, Greg, let alone understand it, if you were going to sell it for me?'

'Good God, no. My personal knowledge and opinion would be completely irrelevant. We would have to agree my compensation.'

'Of course. One can't get owt for nowt, as we say in Yorkshire.'

'Compensation is an interesting euphemism, isn't it? Much used in your world, Denis. "With share options and bonuses, XY's compensation is in the tens of millions." As if work were a sacrifice.'

'Wouldn't you worry about your credibility as an academic?'

'You must be joking. Denis. Academics are

in the same game, but rather pathetically, unless they are scientists, who make real money, and who have to sell their work throughout their working lives. People would associate me with your great ideas, and I would probably be appointed to prestigious academic institutions, and even get prizes, not for my academic work as such, but for my suddenly acquired public charisma. That's the way of the world in academe.'

'How would we start?'

'After we had reached an agreement on my compensation, you could see if you could let me have one or two slogans about your great discovery. It wouldn't matter how much or little they revealed, so long as they were eye-catching and ear-catching and excessive. Would you give some thought to that?'

'I will, and I will get back to you.'

Denis Dobson and Greg Gatsby had met in North Borneo in the way that one so often meets significant new people in one's life, by sheer chance. Gatsby was doing some fieldwork on transgender shamans in indigenous societies. It was funded by the Simone de Beauvoir Institute for Diversity Studies (BIDS). (In the academic world, you don't get anywhere unless you are from an existing acronymic institute or you create a new one. As Professor of Applied Humanism, Gatsby established the Schiller Center for Alternative Meaning (SCAM) at his own university in America which we will not identify here.

Dobson had been less forthcoming about what he was doing in North Borneo. It is possible that he was investigating investment possibilities in the kumquat industry. The two of them met sharing kumquat martinis in the bar of the North Borneo Sofitel. Dobson said that kumquat martinis were the best martinis he had ever tasted anywhere in the world. So a kumquat investment may have been in his mind.

They met on and off thereafter, in various bars from Aberdeen to Zanzibar, usually sharing indigenous cocktails, of which they gradually acquired an encyclopaedic knowledge. They were, in their different ways, men of the world.

They were able to agree on appropriate compensation for Gatsby's prospective contribution to the making of the immortal fame of Dobson, and possibly to some addition to his already considerable wealth. For once, Dobson was not in a strong negotiating position. But he was a businessman on what lawyers call a frolic of his own, outside the normal limits of his business, and money was not a consideration. They agreed to meet at the Ritz Bar in Paris to consume a few more cocktails and to plan the campaign.

'So, Denis, what about some slogans?'

'It's not been easy, Greg. I've thought of three that I might cross your mind with, as a pitch, you understand.'

'I understand. Fire away,'

THE HUMAN WORLD IS HORIZONTAL. A NETWORK OF COMPETING CONSPIRACIES. NOBODY ACTUALLY RULES ANYBODY.

Gatsby hesitated, as if deep in thought. Dobson watched him anxiously.

'I'm blown away, Denis. I don't know what to say. I have no idea what on earth they mean. But that doesn't matter one bit.'

'You like them?'

'Of course not. They're awful. But you're right. They could change the world, starting from tomorrow.'

'How could we functionalise them, do you think?'

'That will require some careful thought. The human mind no longer exists. The communal media have replaced it. So, the functionalising question reduces itself to the problem of the best possible way to use the media.'

'Couldn't we just plaster them all over the media? On the side of buses. On hoardings. Instagram. Facebook. And so on.'

'Heavens, no.'

'What then?'

'We've got to get them talked about first.'

'How can we get them talked about, if nobody knows anything more about them?'

'That's the great secret. I have friends in the media. You have friends in the media. Influencers. We've got to talk to them, telling them that everyone is talking about a new philosophy that makes all other philosophies redundant and which will change the whole world from top to bottom.'

'And will make global poverty a thing of the past, and deal with climate change, and end the scourge of war?'

'Exactly, Denis. You're getting the idea.'

'I thought I'd already got the idea.'

'But an idea is not worth anything until it's functionalised. You are familiar with that in your business life. An investment matures, as it were, when people come to believe what they had been told by those who said that it was a good investment and who buy the wretched thing in great numbers. It snowballs then with its own, totally fabricated, inherent energy. That's what we must aim to do with your new philosophy, or at least with your slogans.'

'I must say it never occurred to me like that, Greg.'

'It's the way of the world, Denis. Or, at least, the benighted modern world of which you and I are unfortunate inhabitants.'

'God bless the Ritz Bar is all I can say, which serves the best indigenous French cocktails, and they are better than any other cocktails anywhere else in the world.'

'Did Denis Dobson have an investment in the Ritz?' Gatsby asked himself but did not ask Dobson.

I hope all of this may help you to understand, dear reader, how you and your friends found yourselves talking about a new world-changing philosophy which would be revealed to the world in all its glory any day soon.

The Sunday newspapers, and even some otherwise intelligent magazines, speculated on the substance of the new philosophy, claiming that they had sources who were already familiar with it. Their accounts differed, of course. But you bought your newspaper or your magazine, and you made your choice. You too could be a provisional expert in the new philosophy.

When people start talking about new ideas at cocktail parties, those ideas have arrived. It happened for A.J. Ayer in the 1930's, Friedrich Hayek in the 1950's, and Ayn Rand in the 1960's.

Denis Dobson was very pleased with his spectacular achievement, while giving unstinted praise to such a brilliant alma mater-pater, whose generous monetary compensation had certainly proved to be fully justified.

You, dear reader, may also begin to have your doubts about the charms of the modern world when I tell you, as I must, that Denis Dobson somehow lost the will actually to publish the full version of his world-changing philosophy. And, as is the way of the modern world and as we all know, people soon found other things to talk about. The Sunday newspapers and the magazines had done well out of it and had moved on.

As Plato, who had Socrates as his alma mater-pater but did not have the benefit of Public Relations, probably did not say: there are always new fish to fry in the fire of human stupidity.

The Dobson entry in the Wikipedia pantheon was surely immortality enough. The achievement of Denis Dobson, well-known but not well understood philosopher and big businessman, was recorded in his obituaries. It allowed him to share in some of the immortality of Ludwig Wittgenstein, well-known but not well understood philosopher and aeronautical engineer.

MORAL
*The market in ideas is as free
as the market in toothpaste.*

* * *

Six

THE INTELLECTUAL'S TALE

HAMPSTEAD HEIGHTS
Metanoia in north London

Serena Stangle reserved her tenderest feelings for her herb garden. A herb garden in Hampstead seemed to her to be something of a triumph and somewhat exotic, like a fig-tree in a remote wadi in the desert. There were also two rather large trees, which had to remain generic, since she didn't know what sort of trees they were. They had green leaves which turned a rather sad yellow in autumn and fell to the ground in despair.

She told people that she retained them to do her bit to save the planet. Trees, you know, de-carbonise even the purer air of Hampstead. She has been known to say that there were times when even a spirit more generous than hers might hope that, by some genetic miracle of mutation, trees could be made to de-carbonise the minds of the lost souls of Hampstead.

Despite her forbidding demeanour, she certainly had tender feelings, otherwise how could she have written a novel that had been reviewed in the London Review of Books, mentioned in the same sentence as Virginia Woolf, which she regretted as a gross injustice to Woolf? She would have preferred a less ambiguous reputation as a George Eliot *de nos jours* or even a Dostoevsky *de nos jours*. But, however creative one may be as a human being, one does not create one's own reputation, does one? We are all waiting for a Julia Kristeva or a Marcel Reich-Ranicki to make or break our reputation, aren't we?

Serena was the sort of woman, of whom we all know one or two cases, for whom every moment, when she is alone, is a negation of something or someone, a fight against the awful tediousness of daily life, and the awful imperfection of one's fellow human beings. In the categories of ancient Greek or Tibetan medicine, it would be classed as bile. She consoled herself with the thought that one cannot be a creative person within an aura of suburban phlegm, can one?

Also, one cannot imagine sharing such a life with a man, of all people, or even a woman, who might turn out to be just as bilious. There were worse things than the life of a hermit, at least a hermit who was productive professionally, in her case in the noble profession of literary creativity.

Only a person of limited comprehension or ill will would dare to call her a desiccated Victorian spinster resurrected. What nonsense! Victorian spinsters did not suffer the twentieth century or attend Oxford University. She was glad that she had taken PPE at Oxford. It had told her all she needed to know, and much more than she wanted to know, about the world made by men, with men. and for men. Not that she was then, or would ever be, what came to be called a feminist. Perish the thought. She is a realist.

She had learned more about herself at Oxford. What other purpose does a university serve? She had learned that she was a right-wing leftist. This makes attachment to a political party difficult. The Conservative Party is too leftist. The Labour Party is too rightist. They're both too feeble and passive. She saw herself as a sort of High Tory Bolshevik, using the best of the past to get rid of the worst of the past.

But she is not in the business of changing the world, the world being irremediably unchangeable. Only once has she taken part in a march on the streets of London in support of her principles.

It was a Brexit Remain march, her view being that the European Union is as bad as all such things are, but it is the work of the Devil to vilify European high culture, of which British high culture is an integral part. The march was disappointing, however. As someone said, it was remarkably like a teetotal cocktail party, or a slow-moving Waitrose queue, a temporary genteel companionship, not liable to intimidate or convert anyone.

She had made some friends at Oxford, it must be said. Not quite like-minded, but equally free and angular spirits. And she still sees them from time to time, and even invites them to her house to share a rational dinner and vigorous conversation. If only the world were ruled by enlightened people. That is the *leitmotiv* of their conversations, but it is capable of an infinite variety of permutations. It may be worth adding that their talk is accompanied by French wines of exceptional quality, of which Serena Stangle is an improbable, you may think, master or mistress. An expression of her equivocal rightism.

Recently, her reputation as a purveyor of rational and well-oiled dinners has spread and, improbably you may also think, her house has become something of a Hampstead salon.

What this costs her in terms of her inherent hermitness is made up for by the feeling that the Paris of intelligent and socially dominant women was for centuries a beacon of European civilisation, from which emerged not only improved versions of, say, Voltaire or Rousseau and many bedazzled English and German visitors. It was also the making of Marcel Proust for whom it was the seedbed, as it were, of a great *fleuve* of a novel, which, according to Serena, has a very good first chapter and a very good last part, and much else in-between. None of us is perfect, are we?

And you, dear reader, are expecting me to reveal now that, in Serena Stangle's Hampstead salon, the love of her life has, at last, made his or her dramatic appearance. No such luck, I'm afraid. Hampstead is definitely not romantic novel country, still less Puccini country.

In Hampstead one is rather more in Henry James country, where no one really understands or cares what anyone else is saying, since all human relationships are intrinsically incomprehensible. Or Tristram Shandy country, where human life itself is nothing but a crazy, comical, fabrication. Shandy did as much as Locke and Hume to unsettle the Cartesianism of the French mind in the eighteenth century but not, fortunately, to put an end to it.

But please don't think of Hampstead as a nest of leftist vipers. Talk of Hampsteadistan on the Hill is far off the mark. Those of the natives who are leftish are, at most, mensheviks with a lower case 'm' and with their fingers crossed. The examples of Trotsky or Gramsci or Rosa Luxembourg were enough to make them see the pointlessness of revolution as a means of social change nowadays.

So what of Serena Stangle's romantic life, if any? You will be glad to hear that one or two people have indeed emerged from the melee. And they are men, and they are not friends from Oxford.

'You have the patina of an old English oak, Serena,' Diego Frontera told her. 'And the delicacy of Dante's multifoliate rose, or the mystical thousand-petalled Tibetan lotus. You are legion. You contain multitudes.'

No one had spoken to her like that before, not even drunken undergraduates at Oxford.

What woman would not surrender some part of her self-sufficiency to regard such talk as merely her overdue due?

'You flatter me, Diego,' Serena said. 'You may be full of the timeless blarney of your Spanish motherland, but flattery is not something we are familiar with in the waste land of the English heart.'

'Flowers bloom even in the desert, Serena. And you are no desert.'

This exchange took place in Serena's salon. It was heard by everyone else who was there. Some of them were also caused to wonder if they too may have been missing something in their lives.

'I have known the unique character of your precious womanhood from the moment that I first saw you,' Émile de Nemours said.

Serena discounted that remark, knowing that Frenchmen never actually mean a word that they say to a woman. What they say is a stylistic convention of lovemaking which is the ultimate French art-form, and the woman knows that perfectly well. It has been an integral part of French manhood since the days of medieval courtly love.

'Dear Serena, you have what Goethe called

the emotional intelligence of the English people,' Siegfried Freud (no relative) said. 'And Goethe was a great admirer of the English people, as I am sure you know.'

'Thank you, Siggy. And some of us women know what a woman doesn't want, even if your namesake didn't.'

Serena wondered for a moment if these men knew who they were talking about, or to whom they thought they were speaking. But only for a moment.

'A woman's place is in the home, as the mother of her children, and the maker of the family-home.'

Only a brave man or an intellectually tone-deaf man could say such a thing in the present company. It was said by Fr. Ed Campion, television personality and the author of *The Joy of Becoming Me* and *My Best Friend God*. He had long experience of the tribes of Hampstead and their folkways. He no longer cared what Hampstead intellectuals might think of his opinions, however *dans le vent* and *tendance* they might think themselves to be.

It was a pleasure for him, and for some of the others who heard what he had just said, to witness the narrowing of the eyes, like cats about to pounce, of these Hampstead folk, as their over-stocked minds Googled a collection of possible responses to what they had just heard.

'That is arrant nonsense, Campion. As you know full well. What century are you living in? A woman may play any role of which she is capable, and which she alone chooses to play.'

'Only in Western society, Gaddi.'

The first responder to Campion's provocation had been Jack Gaddi, an American author of best-selling and crude novels, the cruder the better selling, who started life with his immigrant parents in the lower East Side of Manhattan and had migrated to England in later life to take up gardening and cricket, which are, he said, the pinnacle of civilisation, and not merely western civilisation. They are a global religion minus tiresome gods, he said.

However, he had retained his place in the Dawkins premier league of religious doubters.

The French *salonnières*, in their glory days, had known the joy of hearing the international intelligentsia indulge in intelligent sword play. Serena Stangle was cautiously happy that such a thing could be happening in her own relatively modest home.

Fr. Campion persisted.

'Western society is the first form of society in the whole history of humanity that is not founded on religion. Thoughtful people in the nineteenth century agonised over the question of whether such a thing is possible. The jury is out on that question.'

I will not trouble the reader further with a blow-by-blow account of the discussion on that particular occasion. Conversation is, by its very nature and purpose, evanescent. The story of Serena Stangle's personal development is a much more important matter.

I will only add that the reader should be aware that the participants in her salon were rarely, if ever, academics speaking from specialist knowledge. They were metropolitan intellectuals speaking off the top of their heads. Academics are rarely, if ever, intellectuals.

For Serena, her salon was a voyage of discovery in which she had been forced, again and again, to see herself as others see her. Anyone who has had total control over the making of the persona with which they face the unforgiving world, even if it is a thorny bramble of a persona, such as Serena's, must experience something close to a nervous breakdown when they realise that they have allowed the unforgiving world to intrude, not only into their home, but into the depths of the sacred persona of their Jungian individuating self.

For Serena, it led to a crisis of her womanhood. Has it been the waste of a half a lifetime to refuse to think of herself as a woman among women?

Like many such troubled people before her – Byron, Ruskin, Wagner, Nietzsche, Thomas Mann, Proust, to name only a few – she betook herself to Venice post-haste. The familiar excesses of the Gritti Palace Hotel helped to cosset her body. The spell of Venice, Byron's fairy-city of the heart, set to work on her soul. Paul of Tarsus and Fr. Campion might call it metanoia, that personal self-transforming which comes from the grace of God. A well-bred Hampstead intellectual would call it the cognitive self-therapy of an exceptional self.

In Venice, a sensitive soul wanders through silent *calli* and *campi* that no cruise-ship tourist ever sees. Your soul wanders with you like a friendly shadow. Your turbulent persona slows down, until you stop and stare at the beauty of a worn stone or a decrepit patch of wall.

You touch a gothic well-head standing alone and proud, touched and seen by countless

Doges, by Marco Polo and Carpaccio and the blessed Giorgione and Aldus Manutius and Veronese and Isabella d'Este, prima donna of the Italian Renaissance, and by Palladio and Guardi and Casanova, in the odd moment when he was not elsewhere, and Napoleon Bonaparte. But probably not by Goethe, who responded in an uncharacteristically grouchy way to Venice.

And you see the famous views of the city in a new way, as glorious and improbable as when they have been made into *vedute* painted by great artists, so that people look at the over-familiar views now, without actually seeing them as they really are.

When Serena returned to Hampstead, a village on a hill looking down of London, a village that no one would call a city of the heart, she was certainly different from the person who had gone from there only a short while ago. But how different and in what direction? We who have become her virtual friends are impatient to know the answer.

To clarify one matter straightaway. She felt no inclination to kneel at the feet of Fr. Ed Campion, at whose sympathetic feet many other convalescent people had knelt on their way to the safer haven that is Rome. Also, she had no wish to consort with the intellectual glitterati of central London who shared their self-hatred in communal disdain for those who neither glittered nor were intellectuals and, when the occasion demanded, disdained each other just as bitterly.

Serena Stangle chose another route to a new individuating of her persona.

She volunteered. An economical description of a whole range of activities that involve giving yourself into the service of other people, embracing humility in the face of the enormities of other people's lives.

She would readily admit that neither Oxford University nor the production of novels reviewed by the London Review of Books nor the inbreeding of Hampstead intellectuals had prepared her in any way, not by what the King James Bible calls one jot or one tittle, to become the negation of her former self.

If the reader finds it difficult to believe that such a thing can happen to anyone, let alone the thorny bramble bush that was Serena Stangle, the reader may find it even harder to believe that Serena continued to host her Hampstead salon, more eagerly than ever, knowing that her guests were also people in need, as much as the sick and the homeless and the penniless and the hopeless. They were people who had also lost their souls in living their self-absorbed and self-distorting lives.

Serena has liberated herself from her old self and discovered a self that she had not known before, a better self. She has found her soul, a soul that had been concealed under layers of anguished pride. For the first time in her life, she would open herself to include other people, trying to help them to have a better life, as she tries to make a new kind of life for herself.

Serena Stangle has become serene. Like Murasaki in the eyes of Genji, her soul has the smile of a half-opened flower.

MORAL
No one of is beyond redemption.
Not even supercilious intellectuals.

* * *

Seven

THE AMBITIOUS YOUNG MAN'S TALE

A CHANCER GETS A CHANCE
Beginning to become himself

For a long time, Edgar Sibling has been thinking about the future. He always says that he was born free. An orphan, abandoned by yet another set of insignificant and indifferent foster-parents when he was fourteen, he has lived on his wits for ten years and more.

The time had come to improve his station in life, and to become what he knew he could be. He had considered a life of crime, becoming a Trappist monk. or going into politics. But he didn't want to waste his many talents. So, there he was, on a Eurostar train to Paris, First Class, at someone else's expense.

The advertisement had said: 'Secretary/companion for lady recovering from illness.' The letter from someone in Paris had been on very expensive writing paper and had contained an offer which was admittedly vague, was not obviously illegal, and was financially promising.

The taxi took him to an address in the Avenue Foch which fully lived up to the writing paper. It was a very expensive house indeed.

'I take it that you are an amoral young man, Mr Sibling.'

'Why do you assume that?' Edgar had not expected quite such a direct opening move.

'Decent people don't respond to personal advertisements in newspapers.'

'Do decent people place such advertisements?'

'Perhaps not.'

Edgar was puzzled by Mr Gré. He didn't look like the owner of such a house. He looked like a recently retired, middle-rank civil servant, tired and impatient, in need of a good tailor and a long rest.

'Have you ever met a countess before?'

'Not knowingly, no.' Edgar was, once again, surprised by Mr Gré's dry directness.

On the following evening, he found himself sitting next to a countess at a dinner party of ten people in that same house, which had seemed dark and silent, but had now somehow been brought to bright and warm life.

Mr Gré, who was presiding at one end of the dining table, had been nothing if not economical in his instructions to Edgar.

'I'm not asking much,' he had said. 'The countess left us to live as a recluse in a convent some years ago, determined to spend her last days there. She came back to Paris recently. You will be her friend. That is all.'

Mr Gré would not say more, and the countess herself seemed to share his frugality in the matter of words. She was a dignified woman with pale blue eyes and a sad smile. She was a countess with an aristocratic title which Edgar failed to remember. He could see no obvious way in which his own morality, or lack of it, would be relevant to their improbable relationship. He decided to treat her like the mother he had never known.

Over the next few weeks, in a Paris displaying the cheerful signs of its annual autumnal rebirth, he accompanied the countess in the daily life of an average elderly and wealthy Parisian woman. Each evening, after dinner, he left her at a very private and very expensive hotel in the rue Christine.

'I believe you have worked in an investment bank in London, dealing in the trade in gold.'

Edgar described the working of the London gold market. The countess was pleased and even excited to hear about it.

'Very good,' said Mr Gré, when Edgar reported the conversation to him. 'You should encourage her to talk about such things. Sooner or later, she will have to take responsibility for her own affairs again.'

Edgar's encouragement of the countess led to a surprising result. She extracted a promise of secrecy and proposed a train journey. It took them to Bordeaux, then by hired car to a deserted farmhouse near Hourtin. There was ivy growing in and out of the window-frames and rusty farm machinery filled a farmyard jungle-deep in weeds.

'My family were here during the war,' the countess had said, as if it were a sufficient explanation of their journey.

Edgar, following her instructions, had soon cleared the rubble and broken glass from a rotted wooden window-seat and had prised it open to reveal a flight of crumbling stone steps. He helped her down into a cellar which stretched the length and breadth of the farmhouse. It was cold and damp and smelled of many kinds of decay. Wooden wine-racks had fallen from the walls onto a pile of rusted metal boxes.

The countess said nothing until they were back in the car. 'It was the whole of my father's fortune. You see, we came from Germany before the War. Pictures and jewellery and…' Her voice trailed away. '…and gold,' she said at last.

Two days later, after their return to Paris, Edgar learned that he would not be seeing the countess again. 'She has gone back to the convent,' Mr Gré told him. He was giving Edgar a farewell dinner at Chez Allard. He had clearly been preparing for the occasion with the help of Scotch. But it still seemed almost physically painful for him to offer some sort of personal explanation.

'Might as well tell you now. The Gräfin is my half-sister. Our father was wealthy. Got out of Germany in 1938. Went to France. I was left with an aunt in Munich. Never saw my father again. I was sent to live with English relatives in Geneva. Frieda must know what happened to our property. The only person in the world who does. Millions. Worth millions. Would be now, anyway. She married an Austrian count. Then she got ill. Wouldn't speak to me for years.'

'So I was to be used to recover your inheritance?'

'It was the only hope, the last chance. Now even that chance has gone. She is more distant than ever.'

Edgar saw no reason to tell Mr Gré about the visit which he and the countess had paid, not to Nice as they had told him on their return, but to Bordeaux. There was no need to destroy Mr Gré last hope of adding so much more wealth to his present prosperity. And Edgar would be quite happy to act on some future occasion as a temporary son, if not heir, to the sad and gentle countess.

Twelve months later, he had a telephone call from Mr Gré.

'The countess is dead. Her last wish was that you should have a gold ring which was of special sentimental value to her.'

'That's very kind. I'd be honoured to have it.'

'Mr Sibling, one other thing. In her note to me, she said that the ring was to go to "my dear Edgar, heir to all my secrets." I shall be in London next week. I very much hope that we shall be able to meet and have a talk.'

'That would be very pleasant and could be very interesting,' Edgar said cheerfully.

Joy de Jean Patou. Mrs Ionescu was not a French scent sort of person. And, anyway, his indispensable housekeeper was away for the day, visiting cousins in Clapham. Edgar closed the front-door quietly. He had been visited in his absence. No doubt about that. A good class of visitor, obviously. Regular burglars don't smell of *Joy*.

Not an expected visitor. Not wholly unexpected either. Without a paranoid cell in his body, he had nevertheless been collecting little jigsaw-pieces of puzzlement to form a bigger puzzle which still didn't add up to any big picture.

To prepare for Mr Gré's visit he went to his study. The oily but illiterate Hampstead estate-agent had said it would make a good television-room. But now it was lined with books from floor to ceiling. It looked out onto a garden, a priceless luxury in London, a garden which Edgar is determined to make beautiful.

Above his writing desk there was a painting. Pontormo's Saint Sebastian. A small painting, newly framed. 35 x 35cms. Il Pontormo or, possibly, attributed to Il Pontormo. The valuers at Christie's had hedged their bets. The power of evil over beauty. The power of beauty over evil. Cultivation of the mind. Cultivation of the body. Cultivation of beauty.

And cultivation of a garden, the purest of human pleasures. A particular paradise made by the invisible hand of the gardener under the universal rule of Nature and of God. Edgar removed the painting from the wall and placed it carefully on the floor, face to the wall.

Mr Gré made no comment on the house. That was puzzling in itself. Not many young men lived alone in houses like those in Cannon Place, houses exuding the self-assured family life of the discreetly wealthy. Perhaps Mr Gré was being considerate. Cannon Place was admittedly not the Avenue Foch.

Nor was there any sentimental speech to accompany the handing-over of the Countess's gold ring. Edgar opened the small black box and said 'Thank you. I will always treasure her memory.'

'I wonder if you'd be willing to go to New York for me.'

Mr Gré had apparently not noticed that Edgar was no longer offering himself as a chancer-for-hire. Perhaps he thought Edgar was some sort of squatter on the premises, not someone who would be at home with Italian Mannerist painters. 'You're talking to someone who knows a Pontormo from a Caravaggio,' he wanted to say. Better not.

'To do what?'

'A senior British diplomat needs a nephew for a while. We thought of you.'

So it was 'we' now. Mr Gré had seemed to be a solitary sort of person. Now he was saying that there were more of him somewhere.

'I'm not an out-of-work actor, you know. What makes you think I'd make a good stand-in nephew, however temporarily?'

Mr Gré paused for a moment, allowing his chilly gaze to scan the contents of what Edgar considered to be an exceptionally elegant drawing-room.

'You would know how to behave, wouldn't you?'

Mr Gré gave Edgar a printed visiting card showing an address in the City of London. No name, just an address. In the City, not in or about Whitehall.

'They'll sort out the specifics.'

Twenty-four hours later Edgar was surveying

the congealed mass of the London landscape through the glass-wall of the fifteenth floor of a very tall building.

'Good morning, Mr Sibling.'

Edgar turned round, startled. Three men were standing on the far side of the room, side by side, motionless, looking as if they had been watching him for some time. The temple-guards in the Second Act of *The Magic Flute*.

The three men introduced themselves as Travel, Accommodation, and Money. Edgar would have liked to meet a fourth man called What-the-Hell-This-All-Is. Sensing his inner need, the three men parted, like stage curtains, to reveal a woman.

'Angela Bond will put you in the picture in New York.'

Angela seemed like someone Edgar could be comfortable with. Fiftyish, woollen two-piece suit, flat heels.

Money soothed him with shirts from New & Lingwood and suits from Ede and Ravenscroft. He knew they were good because he looked good in them. He was glad to think that they would help other people to share his understandable pleasure in his own admirable appearance. Travel consoled him with Club

World on British Airways. Accommodation completed the seduction with a suite at the Carlyle on Madison Avenue at East 76th St. Edgar had to admit that there were worse ways of prostituting oneself.

In New York, with Angela Bond's help, he began to understand something of the nature of his mysterious new employment. He was to be an *homme à tout faire*, a general-purpose agent of an allegedly benign international conspiracy of which the elusive Mr Gré was evidently some sort of ring master, and of which members of various national security services, including Britain's MI6, were evidently co-conspirators in their private capacity.

He had been bought. But it was not the happenstance of the countess's gold that decided the matter. Nor was it the fact that, as far as he could understand it, which was not very far, the purpose of the conspiracy was to make the world a better place by non-conventional means.

What decided the matter was that his new employment had already improved his station in life and would probably improve it further. It might even include some welcome elements of crime, monastic isolation, and politics. He will not be wasting his many talents after all.

> MORAL
> To become what you are,
> you need a lot of luck.

* * *

Eight

THE HOLY WOMEN'S TALE

VIRTUE REWARDED
A convent decamps

Sister Monica was a saint of patience and tolerance. That may be why she was Mother Superior de facto of the Holy Mother Convent in Shropshire, England. She has had a lot to be patient and tolerant about. She managed not to look like a nun, with her rosy complexion and lively Irish blue eyes.

The youngest daughter of a large family, she did what had been expected of her. But taking the vows was entirely her own joyful choice. When they hear that someone is from an unusually large family, people often say glibly: 'Catholics', as if there could be only one explanation, ignoring a perfectly natural and worthy philoprogenitive instinct.

People living together in confined circumstances often find that the natural human tendency to annoy one another is much magnified. Astronauts, submariners, university dons in the ancient universities, prisoners, people in Antarctic research stations, people working in star-studded kitchens, husband and wife, close friends. It is a particular problem for monks and nuns, who are unusually conscious of their own failings in case they may amount to sins.

Sister A is tone-deaf but insists on singing rather loudly the Gregorian chant and hymns. Sister B makes a lot of noise when she is eating and drinking, which is not good when the main meal of the day is taken is silence. Sister C cannot sow a straight row of seeds at the right distance apart and cannot clip a hedge neatly. Sister D does wilfully exaggerated gestures of holiness, prolonging genuflections and signs of the Cross and Kisses of Peace quite unnecessarily. Such things, and many others, would try the patience of a saint.

Sister Monica did not have any particular annoying behaviour, but this was itself a source of annoyance for the other nuns, which is why they had come to impose on her the burden of de facto Mother Superior. However, in making her Confession to the priest who came on most days to say Mass, Monica had to admit that she was paying a price for her patience and tolerance. She was repressing a normal human amount of anger and annoyance, and lack of love for one's fellow human beings, and, but for the grace of God, she might one day un-repress it in surprising ways. The priest said that that was not, strictly speaking a sin, and imposed no penance.

There were big decisions to be taken from time to time. The nuns decided by a majority of five to two to purchase a television set, an agent of the Devil if ever there was one. They limited themselves to one hour of television per day, and they said an appropriate prayer before and after.

Eventually, by a majority of eight to three, they decided to purchase a lap-top computer, where the work of the Devil is apparent even to the ungodly. They had it mainly for the e-mail, of which they were each allowed to send and receive one per week. They had not bargained for advertisements for garden sheds and craft gin, let alone for erectile dysfunction.

The alert reader will have noticed that the voting for these things seems to imply that the nuns now not very numerous, unless there had been a whole slew of abstentions, which would probably have been the holy thing to do.

The Convent had been founded by refugees from the French Revolution. The nuns had been known as *mères* until relatively recently (say, 1880). The Convent thrived, thanks to the Continental European addiction to wars and revolutions. It had two 'good' World Wars, nursing people in military hospitals, driving ambulances, taking in children evacuated from London, working as Land Girls.

Then, in the 1960's, the world changed. People started finding their spiritual solace in other places, getting their highs from other sources. Vocations to the priesthood and monastic life lost such attraction as they had had. After the 1960's universal indifference set in, indifference to everything deep or difficult or long-term.

This left monasteries and convents in a problematic situation. Many had to give up the ghost, and close down. The Convent of the Holy Mother carried on, through thin and thin. They had the income from the Convent's farm which had always been leased to a farmer. They found fragile sources of income in baking pies for the local farm shop, in making elderberry wine, and in crocheting tea-cosies and doylies, all of which sold well at the same outlet.

Then they discovered Airbnb. Their many spare rooms could at last be put to good use, with religious services, a chapel, occasional soul-restoring retreats and the extensive gardens as optional extras.

This led to donations from satisfied customers, legacies in wills, and, by the grace of God, a donation from a redeemed sinner, or so he claimed to be, which was a sum not unadjacent to a number in six figures. 'For the beautiful Holy Mother Convent. May it live again in the grace of God.' Improbable as it may seem, a slight ambiguity in that prayer would turn out to have legal significance!

The donor had made money from acquiring failing companies which he then rationalised by sacking as many people as possible, making the companies valuable in a new way, in terms of their hard assets as town-centre property and so on. One might admire his capitalist sagacity, but we can perhaps understand that he might feel a need for redemption.

Their sudden accretion of wealth put the nuns in an unenviable situation. They had to decide collectively what to do with the money.

At first, they did the obvious things. They upmarketed the Airbnbism in small ways, so that the Convent began to take on the character of a boutique hotel. The vague smell of disinfectant and polished wooden floors, not to mention the smell of incense, expected in a convent, began to give way to the various scents of luxury, featuring lavender and rose and lily and cigar.

The nuns themselves hardly noticed what the small incremental steps were producing, until their attention was drawn to an article in the *Sunday Times* saying that the rich and famous had found a place of consolation in the depths of Shropshire. Rather oddly, the headline was 'Peace and Plenty on the River Clun'.

The nuns wouldn't have been able to tell the rich and famous from Adam and Eve. They looked remarkably like other middle-class guests, although admittedly arriving in rather large cars, sometimes with a driver. And one couple did arrive on the back lawn in a helicopter. And they were remarkably generous in their tips, perhaps being unable to tell the difference between the habit of a nun and the uniform of a parlour maid.

The ever-alert reader may have guessed that the Croesus who had caused all this had managed to insinuate a virtual managing agent into the convent in the form of a defrocked Catholic priest who knew his way around convents, not to mention potentially valuable estates.

It is important to stress that the nuns continued their religious way of life and ceremonies, so far as they were physically able to do so. The arrival of a new cook-housekeeper was something that they had been wanting for years. Not to mention the state-of-the art central heating or the total re-wiring, which the nuns knew were long overdue.

Or rather that was true of all the nuns with one exception.

Sister Perpetua, whom it seems right to call by her name, had a relatively late vocation. She came from an Irish American family in the state of Massachusetts in the USA. Her family had done well and were fully accepted in Boston society where they had always been politically active.

Sister Perpetua had taken her J.D. at Georgetown University and qualified as a lawyer. In the best Catholic spirit, she had specialised in pro bono work and civil rights work. She was a notoriously 'good sort'. It came as no great surprise to her family or her friends when she decided to take the veil.

The nuns at Holy Mother Convent, two of whom were now rather close to the joy of meeting their Maker again, were happy to have a young person among them, and a young person who seemed to be a nun with wider perspectives, a nun of the world perhaps.

Sister Perpetua saw what was happening to the convent and, bringing an American mind and American real-world experience, not to say the mind of a lawyer, to the task, began to form her own judgment of what was happening.

It was not quite the judgment that the savvy reader of the present lines may be expecting. The words bribery and corruption were not part of it. Instead, she focused on an interesting, and not straightforward, legal question.

Who owns Holy Mother Convent?

Sister Perpetua was not familiar with English land law or personal property law or contract, but the law of Massachusetts came from the same origin and was probably not dissimilar. She noticed that the few legal documents she could find were all in the name of Holy Mother Convent. So, she thought she could conclude, the convent must be a legal person in its own right. However, it was the nuns who had always acted in its name, making contracts, written and implied, in the name of the convent.

The reader of the present lines may or may not know that what is called the American Realist view of the nature of law says that law is nothing more than a prediction of what a court would decide. She had little doubt that an English court, familiar with the common law as a judge-made law, would be likely to take the same view as a court of the state of Massachusetts, namely that the nuns are, indeed, the legal representatives of the convent, which is to say its owners.

The nuns had the legal right to dispose of the convent, its land, its farm, its buildings and its goods and assets! Unlike the Church of England, the Catholic church in England could not seriously assert ownership of a convent.

A death in the family meant that Sister Perpetua should, in all decency, make a brief visit home. Sister Monica gave her agreement.

To her family she gave a vivid account of the Convent and the extraordinary condition it found itself in, half-convent and half-hotel, tending towards the latter. Her family listened in delight, but not in great surprise.

After two thousand years of the ups and

downs of the Catholic Church, no Catholic was surprised about the turbulent life of its greater and lesser institutions. Much worldwide travelling to spread the Word, countless martyrdoms, several schisms, rival popes, Renaissance virtual monarchs, oppression and repression, and, finally, indifference, at least in Europe. The Roman Church had seen it all.

Sister Perpetua's mother, a no-nonsense Catholic and a woman of the world in many ways, said that she had a bright idea. which might or might not be helpful.

'Why not sell up the whole thing, and move the whole thing to the United States and, why not, to the lovely, and occasionally holy, state of Massachusetts, always in need of much more holiness?'

Sister Perpetua's father, a loyal but sensible Catholic, said that he also had had a bright idea. He knew the owner of a rundown private house which was on the scale of the minor palaces of Newport, Rhode Island, originally created during the Gilded Age at the turn of the twentieth century, when money flowed like the higher reaches of the Mississippi. If his daughter agreed, he could have a word with his friend, the owner of the property.

She agreed, but, please, with no commitment for the time being.

Sister Perpetua shared these developments with the Holy Mother Convent nuns in the most tentative and discreet terms.

The response of Sister Monica, de facto Mother Superior, was not quite what Sister Perpetua expected.

'Must be worth millions. Our generous donor, God bless his troubled soul, evidently has plenty enough money in the bank.'

Sister Monica's repressed disillusionment with the human species had evidently found an appropriate focus.

You, dear reader, may have wondered about what you have heard tell of the New Holy Mother Convent in America, with its many nuns young and old, and about its reputation as the throbbing heart of a great revival of faith and good works extending far beyond its walls, and beyond the limits of the Commonwealth of Massachusetts.

The two oldest nuns from the old Holy Mother Convent decided to stay behind to live out their days in a care-home, paid for by some of the winnings from the sale of the Convent. The other nuns showed a remarkable impatience to leave as soon as possible. They felt that they were being led across the water to a promised land flowing with milk and honey, where they could sing a new song to the Lord.

We know that they are holy women serving God with utter loyalty in the best way that they know, whose sanctity had been violated by an intruder from another world.

The Good Lord works in complicated ways.

MORAL
The bad may be the good in heavy disguise.
Be patient!

* * *

Nine

THE PHILOSOPHER'S TALE

MIND GAMES
Too much information about philosophy

'Fleet Street hacks are getting younger.'
'My boss, Joe Lester...'
'Sent me a grovelling apology for his absence. I must say his debilitating disease seems to have struck rather suddenly.'
'From one day to the next.'
'So they sent the office-boy.'
'I did leave Cambridge with a First in Classics.'
'Which prepares you for what, may I ask, in what is laughingly called the real world.'
'To meet gods and heroes.'
'Huh. I've never met such a person myself, and I have been treading the boards of public inanity for a very long time.'
'Mr Lester sang your praises...'
'It takes a charlatan to know one.'

'But you are one of the best-known philosophers on the planet, apparently.'

'I am a philosopher, apparently, as you say.'

'That is why I'm here. Although I must say I don't really know what a philosopher is in the modern world. Is it a sort of vocation? Or is it a job?'

'It is a vocation or calling. Many are called, but not many get chosen. You're a philosopher if people call you a philosopher. The list of birthdays in *The Times* calls me a philosopher. My CBE is for services to philosophy. It is also a job. You can make money.'

'But there must be some objective test, surely. You wouldn't say a butcher or a car-mechanic or a confidence-trickster is a butcher or a car-mechanic or a confidence-trickster because people say they are.'

'A philosopher also dissects, anatomising other people's minds, tinkering with their inner workings to make them work better, and sometimes we must feed their minds with ideas whose truth value, if any, only the philosopher could say. People would not be far wrong if they call us butchers or car-mechanics or confidence-tricksters.'

At that time, I was working on my first job

at a national newspaper, a low-paid grunt, but richly rewarded with my accumulating experience of the real world and real people, neither of which I had come across at Cambridge. It was something of a coup to be asked to interview John Singer Bunyan. Could that possibly be his real name? It was something of a disaster to have to meet him on my own.

My dear colleagues in the office had told me that JSB was as impossible to interview as a slippery fish. He chews up lesser mortals for breakfast, they said. But more credit to me if I get anything out of him worth putting on paper, to share with desperate readers who might know his name, but know nothing else about him, and for whom an interview with a philosopher would normally be a page-turner in the bad sense, as the newspaper being hurried on its shortest route to the refuse-bin.

'We philosophers call it Nominalism, as you should know, young man. Everything is its name, and nothing more. Nothing exists otherwise. Reality is what is known as reality. I am the man known as John Singer Bunyan.'

'And my pain in the tooth or...a pain in the neck?'

'Imagination. If there were a God, he would not call it a pain in his tooth. It is the fate of us fallen human beings.'

'God's mind is on higher things, surely.'

'Do you claim to know the mind of God, dear boy? Is that from personal contact or from revelation?'

Perhaps JSB himself was nothing but a name. It could explain a lot.

I averted my gaze for a moment to make sure that my recording-machine was switched on.

'Is that why you live in Paris?' I said.

'Why in heaven's name do you ask me such an impertinent question? Philosophers have a private life, like any other public performer.'

'Well, I believe that philosophers are well respected in France, unlike in England.'

'There are philosophers and philosophers. And not all French philosophers are philosophers.'

'What are they then?'

'Celebrities. TV. *Le Monde*. *Paris Match*. That sort of thing.'

'But isn't that a proof of success? They get their ideas through to lots of people.'

'True philosophers are natural hermits. Contemplating eternity and the ultimate truths.

Socrates is our hero. Or Immanuel Kant. Natural loners.'

'But you say you are a nominalist. No eternity. No ultimate truths.'

'We true philosophers are idealist nominalists.'

'Isn't that a contradiction in terms?'

'Life is a contradiction. Death is the contradiction of life. And vice versa. You haven't asked me if I have what might be called my own philosophy.'

'And do you?'

'I don't have a philosophy. I do philosophy. Philosophy is performance art. Each of us is the author, the actor and the audience of our own particular form of sharable madness.'

The time for lunch was approaching. We were due to do the main interview over lunch. However, I must honestly admit that there had entered my mind an unwelcome thought. Lunch is not a tea-party, admittedly. But maybe a philosopher can be aspiring to be seen as a Mad Hatter, using it as an exclusionary tactic. To keep other people out.

We went to the *Deux Magots*. Would my credit-card stand the strain? What on earth was I going to put on my expenses claim?

'Philosophers must show to the world that they are superior people by eating well in public. Don't you think, George? Do you mind if I call you George?'

'It is my name.'

'I'm beginning to think it is also your nature.'

'What on earth is the nature of a George.'

'There were six English kings called George. Enough said, surely. And think of George Eliot and George Sand. They weren't all that they were called, were they? We must all have sympathy for that.'

'Do you regard yourself as religious, Mr Bunyan?'

That was the one question my colleagues in the office said that I must not ask. Our newspaper is profitable, but damages for causing apoplexy to a public figure might strain the budget, including the fees of many Q.C.'s.

The great man smiled, but not in a reassuring way.

'Religion. Ah, religion,' he said pensively. 'Yes. What, one may ask, is religion really?'

'I think it's mythology plus theology,' I said, the classicist in me speaking.

'There's the rub. You must turn your machine off, as I say what I am going to say to you, only to you, what I have not said to anyone else. Do you know what off the record means?'

'Of course.'

But I have to say that I had the feeling that a scoop might be in the offing, recording machine or no recording machine. They would have to start paying me a fair wage in London. Unfamiliar with the machine, I somehow failed to turn it off.

'I began with the Jesuits. The clever sort of priest. Interminable novitiate. I asked one of them if God had perhaps given up on the human race, as a big mistake and a bad investment. They said that, if that's what I thought, Jesuitry was probably not the thing for me. I could take the mythology, the fiction. But the theology was a bit of a challenge. The truth, the whole truth, and nothing but the truth. Oh dear! Dear George. Aquinas and all that. You know what I mean.'

The scoop would be that JSB may possibly be human after all, deep inside all the Mad Hatterism. Vulnerable even.

The B*eaujolais Nouveau* had perhaps begun to loosen a tongue tied for most of a lifetime, for comprehensible professional reasons. Thank goodness it wasn't two bottles of *Château*

Margaux 2015. At least my credit card and my expenses form shouldn't pose a problem, thank God.

We withdrew to the *Café de Flore*. A welcome sight for me was when two humble citizens – probably not humble, actually – approached JSB, bowing and scraping, as one would call it if they really had been humble. At least they didn't ask him to sign a book.

'The French do think that I have a philosophy, George. Their own philosophies are especially convenient. Phenomenology and existentialism and structuralism and post-structuralism and post-modernism and post-postmodernism, and so on. You may nail yourself to one of those masts, and re-nail it elsewhere as often as you like. They are very broad churches, rather like the Church of England, so that everyone can feel at home in all of them. No one need feel excluded.'

'They're not worried about realism and idealism and nominalism, and so on?'

'Good God, no. And they smile superciliously at British empiricism. They know that the natural sciences are fantasy. Imaginary reconstructions of the natural world in words and equations. Philosophy for them is an achievement of the imagination, like painting and sculpture and poetry and novels and the cinema. It's all the same thing.'

'Isn't that what the French think of as culture, as they define the word?'

'And, behind it all, George, is the most absolute cynicism. They don't believe in anything. They never really believed in Christianity. What a relief that must be! They believe what they say, as they say it. And they talk a lot. That's why I live in Paris.'

It was good to see JSB at one with himself at last, at least for the moment.

'Now, let's get down to business,' he said. 'You and me. I'd like you to be my assistant.'

I didn't conceal my surprise at such a preposterous suggestion. I had the presence of mind, however, to dignify it with a rational response.

'You will have gathered that philosophy is not exactly my strong suit,' I said. 'At Cambridge I worshipped at the feet of Plato and Aristotle, and fell in love with Socrates and Plato, as everyone does. But I formed the pathetically immature view that, after them, there was nothing more to be said. That excused my ignorance of all subsequent philosophy.'

'That's not an immature opinion at all. We philosophers know it, even if we don't often say it. After the ancient Greeks, there's really nothing more to be said. We can't tell people that, obviously. It would put us out of business.'

'What about Descartes and Spinoza and Locke and Hume and so on?'

'All been said, long ago. Think of Wittgenstein. Poor chap. Mind you, he'd given away his inherited wealth, so giving away philosophy may not have seemed a big deal. When he was young, he said that the only truth is scientific truth. There's nothing more to be said. Later he said there are different truths for different mind-games. Socrates knew that. Science and religion and so on. Just as there are different rules for chess and cricket, and there's nothing more to be said. Thank goodness women are too sensible to play the philosophy game. Philosophy is a man's game. If women do join in, they become temporary men, and lesser women. Women are best as psychologists, humanising Freud and Jung and Adler and the rest of that *galère*.'

'The French are very keen on Wittgenstein, aren't they?'

'For the French, philosophy is a fashion item. Styles come and go. *New Look. Nouvelle vague. Nouveau roman. Nouvelle cuisine. Nouveaux philosophes.* Skirts go up and down, and screen plays, and novels, and sauces and ideas.'

'So what would I be expected to assist you in doing exactly, Mr Bunyan.'

'Oh, please call me Bunny. My friends do, such as they are. I have it in mind to invent a new religion. A sort of *dernier cri de cœur* for the beleaguered human species.'

'A new religion. That wouldn't go down well even with the French, would it?'

'It will be a religion that worships beauty. Plato and Christianity and the Renaissance and all the other Enlightenments were really about the worship of beauty. The beautiful is the good as a moral aspiration, but without the guilt. Tailor-made for the French, don't you think? High-fashion philosophy, if ever there was one. *Nouvelle foi.*'

'Sounds more German to me, Bunny.'

'More Chinese, I think, dear boy. Confucius tells the Chinese to see philosophy as a bit like religion without the rituals, something to make a better life in society, while respecting the powers-that-be.'

'I see,' I said, meaning that I had no idea what he was really thinking.

'You should love my new religion, George. The love of beauty is the only thing that can raise us above the animals. You must be my St Paul, helping to spread the word.'

'But surely we live in a world that worships money and evil and indifference and mutual hatred?'

'Could there be a better time to spread the word of the love of beauty as the only good-in itself? *Das Gute an sich*, as the Germans say. Could there be a place more in need of some new enlightening than the awful world as it is, a world that pretends that it's a civilised world? *Die Welt als ob*, as Hans Vaihinger so rightly said. The world as fiction. Pretty bad fiction, at that.'

Maybe I could see his point or, more precisely, I could see where he was coming from, as the Americans say to avoid commitment. But, getting on board the good ship Mad Hatter the Second, might not be a good career move on my part.

'I am deeply honoured by your suggestion that I might be able to help you, Bunny. Can I have a little time to think about it?'

'Of course, dear boy. Remember that God works in mysterious ways, not least the God of Beauty.'

'I will try to remember that.'

Joe Lester was very understanding of my failure to produce a few hundred well-chosen words for the Sunday paper.

'Truth is, George, it was meant to be a bit of an initiation rite for you. The average celebrity is not difficult to interview, but for a different reason. They believe that they are what their public relations people tell them that they are. You just have to write it down, spiced with an aura of irony that the celebrity in question wouldn't be able to detect. You soon learn how to do that. It makes us, and the reader, feel superior to the deeply unsatisfactory people we assist in their miserable self-promoting. They're always plugging something, even if it's only their non-existent selves.'

'Bunny Bunyan is definitely savvier than that.'

I did not tell my boss that, initiation rite or not, it has led me to consider my position, as politicians are told to do, when people mean that they should resign.

You probably don't get more than one

opportunity to change the world. Is this mine? Or am I just the latest victim of Bunny Bunyan's calculated professional lunacy?

MORAL
Everyone can be their own philosopher.
Give it a try!

* * *

Ten

THE IMMORTALS' TALE

PANDORA'S OTHER BOX
Time past is time present

I saw Oedipus several times at Patrick Lane's house on Corfu. He and Jocasta were on some sort of trial separation. He seemed a bit more relaxed, like Atlas with the weight off his shoulders or Sisyphus having a breather, in the words he himself used to describe his state of mind at that time.

Even so, I can't say he was a bundle of laughs, at least not laughs of the laugh-out-loud kind. He certainly had a never-ending fund of stories about the old times, but often rather crude and cruel. Mount Olympus meets the Catskills.

I remember once when Gertrude Stein was there. Sans Toklas. Oedipus arrived out of the blue in an ancient Rolls Royce Phaeton, with a strikingly good-looking Ganymede-type as his personal driver. Patrick, knowingly, invited

Oedipus to sit beside Gertrude. They hit it off straightaway.

Both of them world-class name-droppers, they were soon into more or less scurrilous reminiscing. Both of them had moved in circles where everybody who mattered knew everybody who mattered. There was a lot to be scurrilous about. People of Ms Stein's kind always washed up sooner or later on the immemorially irresistible shores of Greece.

Such people had led usefully complicated and mostly disastrous lives, in fact or as processed in the myth-making mills of their own minds and other people's minds. Many of them earned their modest crust from their overactive imagination shared with others. Everyone is two people. Their self and their myth. These were people who had become their myth. Ms Stein and Oedipus were two of a kind.

Meeting a transcendental ancient Greek, as it were, meant that Ms Stein was in her own blissful seventh heaven. Ouzo and retsina helped her but not Oedipus, who was teetotal in an assertive sort of way, like a reformed alcoholic who had known only the best sort of drink in his day, so that abstinence now was not so difficult. And he, of course, had known a different Greece, to which, as Byron said, another inveterate name-dropper, we owe now a blush and a tear.

I feel I should make some attempt to share with you the consensus, the public opinion, as it were, of such wildly unrepresentative human beings. To be honest, I don't think their opinions matter very much. The opinions of a self-appointed and self-absorbed elite didn't matter very much then. Today, they would count for less than nothing when the human mind is in slavery to the madness of an electronic mass mind, a work of the Devil which should make into believers those whom the Devil makes into doubters of his existence.

But these people who met under the ever-shining sun and the ever-blue sky of Greece, were there, above all, to talk, which they were accustomed to doing unstoppably throughout their lives. For such people, to live is to talk. And they were much more individual and quixotic than the human average, so that their states of mind have an anecdotal, not to say an anthropological, fascination of their own.

Their attitude to war, for example. Oedipus had had a good deal of first-hand experience of war, as had Patrick Lane. The ruling class had fought in the First World War, like in the

Crusades. Many had been killed. The children and grandchildren of the veterans bore a sort of war-guilt, a survivor-guilt, as they charlestoned away their meaningless lives in the nineteen-twenties, and as they fell into more or less genteel poverty in the nineteen thirties.

I remember an occasion when Oedipus was not there, but Ovid was there, a namedropper if ever there was one. He knew more about the goings-on of Oedipus and his ilk than they knew themselves, and certainly more than anyone else whom one could invite to lunch. What about all the awful worst, done by so many of the otherwise best of people, including gods, senior and minor?

Ovid said that, after long and careful thought, he had decided that the prevalence of evil was all due to natural selection, genetics and the early life of the child. Or, as he put it in less anachronistic terms, out of the womb into the tomb. The others nodded sagely, able to recognise the possibility of truth when it occasionally crossed their path.

Patrick was proud to have got the Kaiser Wilhelm and Robert McNamara among the guests on one memorable occasion.

'We didn't sleepwalk into the First World

War,' the Kaiser said, in impeccable English. Devoted grandson of Queen Victoria, whom he held in his arms at her death in 1901, but no friend of her successor, his uncle Edward VII.

'We had been marching towards war for fifty years. It was the idea of the destiny of a German *Volk* as a world power, its *Weltberuf* that had united Germans since 1848 under the leadership of my own dear Prussia. Everyone knew that the rival alliances at the turn of the century could lead to war. And we Germans saw a possible collateral benefit of war if it put an end to the arrogance of the British Empire.'

'We Americans made a new world order after World War Two,' McNamara said, 'with a collateral benefit of substituting an American Empire for the British Empire, in the name of our own Manifest Destiny, which is all that unites us a nation. We didn't know what we were getting into in Korea or Vietnam, or that we would be helping China to become a great power. Everybody knows that if the brilliant system of the post-war world order falls apart, there will be another Cold War, and possibly another world war.'

The less exalted guests on this occasion also seemed to be especially conscious of their own past lives, including, in several cases, the fact that they had somehow managed to avoid the Second World War. They were not so much conscientious objectors as transnationally mobile, managing to survive in the south of France or Spain or the United States, often in the company of other displaced persons. To be deprived of your London club or the Ritz bar or Bayreuth or Le Procope was a reasonable ground for self-pity, even if you could not expect the pity of others.

On another occasion, there was talk about mythmaking, national and personal.

'I became my myth,' Thomas Mann said, wistfully. 'It was never the real me.' The other guests nodded sagely. Most of them knew that they too had become their myth. It was a source of pride and income. And so they are immortal. They will never die. Mann's all-embracing wistfulness was a patented product, and very much a source of income.

Jean Cocteau was not one of Patrick's favourite guests. He had always been his own myth. He didn't need to become it. He enjoyed it. He even liked a two-edged joke about himself. What is the plural of Cocteau? Cocktails. He re-invented himself from moment to moment and, admittedly, that was a fascinating thing to see for a spectator.

His social duty of causing shock would have been more attractive if it had been more like that of Nietzsche, for example, whose relentless provocative self-giving, with a hint of irony, was really a sharing of existential anxiety.

Patrick had tried to get Nietzsche to visit, but he said that sunshine and blue skies were not his thing. He failed with Freud too, who said much the same thing. Patrick had wanted Freud to meet Oedipus.

Another remarkable occasion was when the guest-list included Oedipus and Martin Luther! Gertrude Stein was also there on that occasion. We had been at a literary do in Marmara. We travelled to Corfu together.

Luther was his usual dyspeptic self. He kicked off by asking Oedipus if he had known Antigone who, Luther said, seemed to embody in herself the ultimate problem of the human world, namely, the problem of evil occurring in a social setting.

Oedipus said that Luther might be thinking of Antigone seen through the eyes of Sophocles. He had once met Sophocles at an evening party and congratulated him on the play. But he told him that he had been too kind to Creon, who was an out-and-out rogue, as Oedipus knew to his cost. Oedipus had known Antigone well. She was a powerful woman among powerful men.

Gertrude Stein, as irrepressible a provoker as Luther, said that Antigone was a victim of patriarchal society and patriarchal law, like Phèdre or Madame Bovary or Anna Karenina. Oedipus said that women were not free of the sin of pride. If they didn't like the world they lived in, they should not blame their misfortunes on everyone other than themselves, as if the world must be reconstructed to suit them.

'Imagine if someone were to say that it was Helen who had launched the Trojan War.' Oedipus said. 'Wife of the long-suffering Menelaus, whom she wronged in such a dreadful way, even if she did go back to him eventually, as Homer generously supposed.'

Patrick asked Luther if he still believed that we are all doomed, no matter how good we are. Luther got a bit agitated. He said that Patrick might not fully understand that neither he nor Luther nor Oedipus nor Francis of Assisi could change the will of God. His will is absolute. Ms Stein said that that was ridiculous. You can't solve the problem of evil by saying that only God can solve it. Even Oedipus had not, presumably, met God. Oedipus confirmed this.

As the meal progressed, the delicious food and wine took its effect on the antagonists who calmed down a bit. For a few moments, there was even a silence filled with almost audible intense thinking. Eventually, Oedipus said, very quietly, that he wanted to share with us something that he found it difficult to say.

When he had met Sophocles at that unforgettable evening party, he had said another thing to him. With tears in his eyes, he had thanked the great man for what he had said about the time that Oedipus had spent at Colonus, when he was at last redeemed for all the many sins of his life by his submission to the higher order of the universe.

Sophocles said that they all owed so much to the divine Socrates and to Plato, his brilliant protégé. Without them, there was no hope of ever discovering a solution to the problem of evil that had made human beings into enemies of themselves.

It may be that I should say a little about how all these things came to happen at Patrick Lane's house.

Patrick had once met Immanuel Kant in a beerhall in Munich. He was on a day trip from Königsberg, not mentioned in his biographies. After a stein or two of beer, Kant succeeded in convincing Patrick that time is an illusion created by the human mind. Everything from the past is eternally present. Everyone from the past is eternally present.

Maybe T.S. Eliot had met Kant somewhere sometime. Kant said that he had always liked his friend Nietzsche's idea of eternal recurrence. Patrick saw at once that this offered new possibilities for hosting interesting parties.

He told Kant that he had been told much the same thing by a guru he had known in India who said that, if there had been no such things as human beings, then what seem to us to be the past and the future would all exist together in an eternally present moment.

Paddy then got in touch with me believing, on slender evidence, that I am better-read and more knowledgeable. He asked me to organise some eternally recurring gatherings at his house. An Eternally Recurring Zoom, you might say, but without the virtuality. Magic idealism is surely a more useful genre than magic realism.

There was something else that Oedipus said on this occasion. He said that he had not known Hesiod who had invented the story of Pandora's box. Gertrude Stein asked Oedipus, with a sarcastic edge to her voice, if he had known Pandora. It might have been useful if he had. Oedipus laughed heartily. How old do you think I am, dear lady?

Hesiod was obsessed by the idea of the decline of humanity from a golden age, at a time when Greece was about to take off into a new age which would, ever since, be admired. Pandora and her box full of human evils gave a convenient explanation of what Hesiod saw as human decline.

However, Hesiod had failed to mention that, in fact, Pandora had had a second box, full of human goods. She opened this box in windy weather, and the human goods flew out, spreading everywhere. Then, when she thought the box was empty, a whole mass of human hopes flew out, and reached the four corners of the world.

Oedipus had been told about this by an impeccable source, namely, Zeus himself in a vision. The result was that, like the myth of original sin, the incomplete myth of Pandora's box had become immortal, serving as a perverse consolation for the self-harming and self-destroying human race.

Oedipus asked whether we knew that the human species can become whatever it chooses to be, beast or god. We said that some valiant people had known this in Jerusalem in the first century. And some people had known it in Florence in the fifteenth century. We said that we would certainly bear it in mind.

MORAL
*A midsummer day's dream
can happen any day.
Enjoy it!*

* * *

Eleven

THE FRENCH WOMAN'S TALE

A FRANCE MORE PROFOUND
Love at last in Quercy

Marie-Hélène had a car with Paris number plates. One should not allow people to forget one's standing in society. She tied her Jean Patou scarf loosely around her neck, to show that it was a thing of beauty, and nothing more. She had a peculiar accent that evoked the highest reaches of education and sophisticated conversation.

Why did she make the effort? She had an aristocratic background of which the peasants were well-aware, their ancestors having touched their forelock to her ancestors for centuries. Her chateau had seen better days, but whose chateau has not. So all of it must have been directed at the local bourgeoisie whose ancestors had made the French Revolution, and whose manners and way of life and arrogance were a permanent affront to decent people.

Like France itself, she relived the French Revolution every day of her life. Rousseau *versus* Voltaire. Voltaire *versus* Rousseau.

She organised small art exhibitions and poetry readings and lute recitals, but she had to concede lengthy intervals for the audience to refresh themselves in a nearby café.

Her ancestors had ruled the village when Aquitaine was ruled by the English. She wondered whether it had been a mistake to let the English go, when France grabbed Aquitaine after a war that took a hundred years to win. The English had not had a revolution, had they? They had not had the correct social order stolen from them by force, had they?

Her country life was a hard life which she had made tolerable by writing several novels. Her novels were not about social superiority, at least explicitly. Like most French novels, they were about the eternal French concern with the finer points and infinite subtleties of what the French call *amour*. Not something that troubles the English, apparently. She thought of herself as a latter-day George Sand or Colette. But her self-esteem didn't need the sustenance of prizes.

Even bastions of the old order need money, however. She had a well-paid job as an editor in a leading publishing house in Paris. She had sold the land on which a supermarket was placed. She had a useful rental income from a flourishing *Centre Equestre* located on her land two kilometres away from the village. Her village had been included in the, admittedly rather lengthy, list of *les plus beaux villages de France*, which probably brought in some serious-minded pilgrims, on the way to Moissac and ultimately to Santiago de Compostela.

From all this one might suppose that the life of Marie-Hélène Biron, marquise de Quercy, was at least a coherent life. But we know enough of human lives to know that the life of a human being is never coherent.

Had she ever opened her heart to anyone? Fully. Other than her mother. She would say no. But she may not be the most reliable witness. For a woman of a certain kind, feelings are inseparable from ideas. For a woman of a certain age, ideas are better remembered than feelings. And she would not see again her forty-second year.

In her adult life she had had two companions. One was with her for three years, the other for seven, which may seem to imply some progress in his or her maturity. But that would be a false inference. As one gets older, we increase our capacity to make everything into a routine, and our capacity to break free from a situation that has lost its savour declines. We settle for what we happen to have. Before we know it, we have taken on the shape of old bedroom-slippers.

Was Marie-Hélène perhaps a political woman in her maturity? She had been political in her immaturity, as everyone is. Her politics has been immature, as became her age and her social circumstances, which inclined her neither to march in the streets to change the world nor to worship the order of things as they are.

Her student friends in the *rue d'Ulm* were impatient with her, even if she had concealed from them her aristocratic roots and the burden of history that she felt as a weight on the still slender shoulders of her personality. Her friends probably thought that her blood was not blue blood but thin blood. And that is a sin for a person of intellectual distinction who should nevertheless be fired by the broad horizons of the young mind. In 1968 she was not a 1968 person.

She was not a political person, in the sense of party politics. Or rather she would say that she was the only member of her own political party. In local elections, she votes for a ruralist party, defending rural traditions. In national elections, she abstains affirmatively.

The problem is that you may detach yourself from politics, but politics will never detach itself from you. Marie-Hélène and her like-minded friends in Paris had a new worry. They were convinced that a new revolution was emerging in France, a silent revolution, a revolution by stealth. The French Revolution had been a chaotic revolution, but at least it had been a bourgeois revolution. The new revolution seemed to be a populist revolution, a people's revolution. Not only was the hierarchical order of France at stake. The very nature of France as a distinct form of civilisation was under threat.

It goes without saying that her like-minded friends were of a conservative disposition, but they were deeply opposed, as she was, to right-wing glorification of an imaginary nation threatened by Islamic immigration. For them, France was something more real and more profound and more resilient than the product of the temporary side-effects of passing events. France had survived the slings and arrows of fifteen hundred years of turbulent history. It had become tough in its very fabric.

But populism was another matter. France had no experience of it. Liberal democracy of the American or English kind might lead the people to suppose that they had some God-given right to a place in government. It was intelligent to console them with that myth. It was not intelligent to take the risk that they might believe it. France had never taken such a risk.

What exactly is Marie-Hélène relationship with her like-minded friends? Her publisher's office is in the rue Jacob, and her apartment is a few footsteps away in the rue de l'Université. Her friends, she would have to admit, are not drawn from any much wider urban area, hardly extending beyond Montparnasse or Saint-Sulpice or Montmartre.

But then they do not see themselves as representative of anything other than their class, the over-educated class, and their professions, which are overwhelmingly intellectual or artistic or both. In short, they could hardly be less representative of the people of France.

And yet, one must also say, people like them have a disproportionate influence on the public mind of France, through their writing in newspapers and magazines, in novels and documentary essays, and through their carefully chosen appearances on television.

Could one say that they were entitled to their influence in a supposedly modern liberal democracy? What was the nature of their friendship among themselves? Did they conspire over a cup of coffee or a decently opulent meal? More important, were they real friends or only functional friends?

One must ask this question as it relates to Marie-Hélène Biron herself. She had become a woman without any true friends, let alone lovers. But at the time we are speaking of here, she was a woman who, improbably, was about to fall in love with a younger man. And that event might have an effect not only on their future but also on the future of France, as still more improbable as that may seem.

She had met Yves-Matthieu at a social event. It was not a *coup de foudre* so much as an instantaneous electric connection, like switching-on a table lamp or an electric heater, a sudden exchange of light and warmth. He was the mayor of a small town near her village.

He was from what people persist in calling a modest background. His father was a gendarme. His mother was a piano-teacher. His talents and determination had taken him to the Lycée Louis-le-Grand in Paris, then to the Sorbonne where he specialised in French economic history, and then, by a well-worn path to the National School of Administration (ENA). He was that creature of myth and resentment, an *énarque*.

Passing out of ENA sufficiently highly on the list of merit, he had taken up a post in a government department which, by one of the mysteries of French government, still allowed him to become a mayor without giving up his official employment. As with the Prefects of the Departments, the job of a mayor is seen as more administrative than political, but a mayor is elected in a local election, rather than being imposed by Paris.

This has meant that, in many cases, the people could have as their local leader someone of high intelligence and with strong links to the notoriously centralised government of France in Paris.

In his late thirties, he too was ready for some change in his personal life which had been constrained by his ambition and excessive devotion to his work. He was good-looking in a way that sensible women prefer, not intimidating or tiresomely seductive. His body was younger than his age due to his obsession with the game of squash, which has the advantage over the game of lawn tennis that it is not seasonal and is usually urban and very quick.

The couple could spend time together in Paris and at Marie-Hélène's country house. Soon the affection of good friends became the love of lovers. *I am in love.* From time to time, she said these words to herself out loud, as if to remind herself of their improbability.

Falling in love involves a series of surrenders for a woman of her age and her kind. She surrendered the fierce pride in her origins, which were, after all, a chance circumstance. She surrendered her self-constructed isolation from strong human ties, an isolation which was also as much a product of circumstances as of her own choice. She surrendered her isolation from political commitment which had been a sign of weakness rather than of strength. She surrendered her own idea of her identity as a unique person. There is nothing more ordinary than being in love.

She even accepted the idea of marriage, having resisted the idea of subordination to any other human being. She even accepted the possibility of becoming a mother, having not felt an ounce of maternity in her self-made self.

Most significantly, she surrendered her image in the minds of her like-minded friends. Their friendship had always been peculiarly formal, lacking the warmth of English and American male and female friends, fuelled by laughter and provocations and drink. Her like-minded friends saw her now as a lost soul, but she did not fail to detect a streak of jealousy that belied the severity of their judgment.

Together Yves-Matthieu and Marie-Hélène set about making her country house habitable. As a child she had inhabited it with her parents, although it had been, strictly speaking, uninhabitable. In a spacious salon on the first floor, with wide views over the timeless countryside, the couple had their own writing desks, set apart, where they could read and write under a vow of silence, saving their conversation for the time when they were preparing and eating their meals together.

She was writing a history of France, assisted by Yves-Matthieu's remarkable range of knowledge. It was not an academic book, but a book for ordinary people to read. It was not lyrical but realistic, seeing her country as if seen by an outsider coming to France, after the model of Montesquieu or Voltaire, sharing their powerful underlying polemical purpose.

That was to be her response to populism and the threat to France's immemorial essence. That was to be the expression of the political commitment that the couple shared.

Unwillingly and unfortunately, they could not avoid becoming a fashionable couple, even what the Americans call a power-couple. Their political commitment obliged them to appear occasionally on television, and to be interviewed by carefully selected newspapers and magazines. It was a surrender of their dignity. They were determined not to allow it to corrupt them, or to damage their primary identity as a loving couple. They had absolutely and finally rejected the idea of seeking political office, and the cruelly ambiguous power that goes with it.

It has seemed right to tell this story of one woman's life, not in the spirit of a *people* magazine, but in a spirit of hope for every woman who is looking for hope and for love, and in a spirit of hope for the everlasting loved one whose name is France.

MORAL
*Mind and food and love trump
liberty and equality and fraternity.*

* * *

Twelve

THE HOLY MAN'S TALE

RE-THINKING IN TRANQUILLITY
Between the past and eternity

'Have you ever met a cardinal before?'

'In my dreams. Literally.'

'You dream about cardinals?'

'More than once. I dreamt I was kneeling in front of a cardinal, in his scarlet robe and scarlet hat. I tried to kiss his ring, but he wouldn't let me.'

'Heavens!'

Jean Grant's original question had been meant as an offer of ecclesiastical advice, not an enquiry about the secrets of Dorothea Dorn's unconscious mind.

'I should probably have worked out a Freudian interpretation, but I thought it would be better not to try,' Dorothea continued.

Jean tried to suppress even the thought, let alone the image, of Dotty Dorn – cheerful, charming, intelligent, and very evidently a vigorous and healthy young woman – kneeling in front of any man, let alone a cardinal.

'I really don't think you need to do any of that for Cardinal Castelfranco,' she said, steering the conversation back in the ecclesiastical direction. 'They make a point of informality nowadays. But Alvise Castelfranco is definitely not a blue jeans sort of person.'

'God! I should hope not,' Dorothea said. 'What's the point of being a prince of the Church, if you're not willing to be princely?'

Terra firma in Venice never seems very firm. You step from the precarious watery medium onto fourteen centuries of impossible defiance. You hope that the blessed miracle – the marriage of denatured sea and unnatural land – will last a little longer.

The two women were helped from the taxi by a man who was apparently some sort of butler, wearing a green baize apron.

'*Grazie,*' Jean said.

'*Grazie,*' she said again, as the man helped her onto a steep stone step, abrupt frontier between intense light and intense darkness. Sensing that the man was treating her as if she were old and in need of physical help, she felt a stab of anxiety. Would the Cardinal think that she was only there as some sort of chaperone because she had thought that Dorothea would need a chaperone when visiting a priest?

Cardinal Castelfranco was not wearing jeans. He was all in black, looking improbably, and probably unintentionally, fashionable. He was evidently in that stage of agedness when a man, or a woman, seems ageless, the processes of growth and decay having agreed to call it a day.

'My dear ladies,' he said. 'You make a very old man feel very much younger.'

The Cardinal spoke English with the best of English accents. But his manner was uniquely Italian, managing to suggest, as no Englishman would be able to suggest, that the very act of shaking the hands of these two strange women was itself one of life's particular pleasures.

'It's so good of you to let us intrude in this way,' Jean said.

'You are here because you see me as the latest in a long line of saints and sinners whose words and deeds are as fascinating as my own are insignificant.'

'To tell the truth,' Dorothea said, trying not to sound either too girlish or too forward, 'as I said in my letter, I am hoping you'll be able to help me solve a sixteenth-century mystery.'

The Cardinal led them into a room dominated by enormous windows looking out over the Grand Canal, but in which there nevertheless seemed to be very little light. The small panes of yellowed glass in the windows were evidently designed to keep out the sunlight without interrupting the view.

'As you already know, Fräulein Dorn, the sixteenth century was not an altogether happy time for Venice or for my family…'

'Or for the Church…'

'Ah! The Church…'

The Cardinal filled the pause with an almost imperceptible gesture that managed to communicate quite clearly an unsighed sigh and the shrugging of unshrugged shoulders.

'The Church…'

Another pause.

'When was there ever a happy time for the Church?' the Cardinal said at last.

The servant in the green baize apron had brought lemonade in two-handled, almost translucent porcelain mugs, with amoretto biscuits on matching plates. The gleaming oak floorboards squeaked pitilessly under the painstaking tread of his feet. The room smelled reassuringly of beeswax, like the parlour of a convent. The fruit of much labour done, no doubt, as a form of prayer.

'Robinson's Barley Water,' the Cardinal said. 'The essence of old England, don't you think?'

Dorothea decided that the time had come to state her case.

'As I think you know, my idea is that Venice had an opportunity in the sixteenth century to restore the unity of Christendom. That means, you had not only religious reasons but also diplomatic and pragmatic reasons for wanting to end the divisions.'

'If we did think that, then it was a strange – and I must say uncharacteristic – fantasy.'

'If I'm not mistaken,' Dorothea persisted, 'a member of your family visited the Emperor in Leipzig in 1550. A lost opportunity – a last opportunity, perhaps.'

'What a marvellous might-have-been!' Jean said. 'No Wars of Religion, no Thirty Years War, no World Wars, no European Union.'

'An impossible might-have-been, I'm afraid,' the Cardinal said. 'As Erasmus said, war is a savage insanity of which human beings seem unable to cure themselves. There will always be those who find reasons for war, he said. And they are as criminal as those who cause the killing.'

The Cardinal led his two guests through a nest of rooms of different shapes and sizes. In one room, there were windows looking onto a *campo* filled with sunlight.

The room was lined with metal shelves. Files and boxes were piled on the shelves and on the floor.

'Whatever there is in here is yours to discover, Fräulein Dorn. I hope you will not be disappointed, but I fear that you may be.'

They returned to the reception room. The Cardinal led them out onto the balcony. Venice perennially observed. Venice perennially indifferent to those who observe it. Venice about which it has been said that nothing can be said that has not been said before.

'Your Eminence, there is one other thing I should tell you,' Dorothea said suddenly.

'My dear child…'

'I believe that a member of my own family was also at that meeting in Leipzig – a distant relative…'

'Then we must share the responsibility, your family and mine, for so many crimes and follies

– the crimes and follies of subsequent European history.'

The Cardinal's voice now had a steely edge, reminding the women that he had spent the whole of his active life at the centre of power of the system of global power that is the Church of Rome.

'And, my dear child, since you have told me something that I did not expect to hear, I will tell you something remarkable that you did not expect to hear when you ladies so charmingly offered to grace me with your presence here today.'

Jean and Dorothea had certainly not come to see the Cardinal expecting to be told anything portentous.

'In my old age, I am more or less a free man – free of all my former responsibilities, even of all my former loyalties – other than the life-long duties of the priesthood, and the loyalty that is the loyalty of every child of God. And so I am free to think, to think for myself. Old men forget, as Shakespeare made Henry V say, but sometimes we are made to think about the past, not wistfully or bitterly, or hopelessly. But we prefer to think about the future. I look for, and long for, another Reformation. And a better response by the Church. But, this time, we must use religion to see beyond religions. The future of God's creation depends on it.'

'You are able to see light in the awful darkness of our times?' Jean said, with surprise and uncertainty in her voice.

'*Ecco! Lux in tenebris.*'

'And if the darkness will still not comprehend…?'

'That is our God-given task, dear Mrs Grant, as it ever was. The divine spark in the human soul cannot be extinguished.'

Dorothea Dorn registered an irony. She, a young scholar, was an avid spectator of the tragicomedy of the human past. The ancient Cardinal had his weary eyes fixed upon a better human future.

The Cardinal bade farewell to his two visitors as graciously as he had received them. He told Dorothea that she should feel free to work on his family archives as and when she wished.

Jean and Dorothea remained silent on the journey back to the Pensione La Calcina. Not that they were not thinking, each in her own way. Dorothea was seeing in Venice the thrilling presence of the elusive past. When you are young, the future is, by comparison, a mere abstraction. Jean was seeing in Venice the illusion of the past, the ambiguity of the present, and the obscurity of a frightening human future.

'Now is come a darker day,' she said quietly, wanting Dorothea to hear, but half-hoping that she would not.

The choppy water of the Canal lapped against the sides of the Cardinal's gondola, the familiar scenes gliding slowly past, the conscious mind at the mercy of the swaying of the jet-black boat, cradle and coffin, unconscious archetype of our first helplessness and our last.

Cheerful uncomplicated Dorothea was not liable to be tempted by metaphysical ruminations. However, as a scholar and historian, she was very much interested in religion. And so, unsurprisingly, was Cardinal Castelfranco. The Cardinal had graciously invited her to meet him on the following day on the island of San Lazzaro. He had an ulterior motive for doing do.

Fifteen minutes by *vaporetto* from the centre of Venice, the monastery on the island of San Lazzaro had played an important part in the Cardinal's life. For George Gordon, Lord Byron, the monastery had been a refuge from his *terra firma* dissipations. For Cardinal Castelfranco it was a physical refuge from the intensity, the complexity and the ambiguity of Rome and Venice and the Universal Church.

It had been a spiritual refuge also, where Alvise Castelfranco could be himself, without titles or responsibilities, alone with the only person who could see him as he really was, the person in whom he believed and trusted as he believed and trusted in no-one or nothing else.

He would share a picnic lunch with the young Austrian in the gardens of the monastery, sharing a stone bench, protected from the sun by the leafy branches of a cool green arbour. The bright eyes of this woman were seeing the intensity, the complexity and the ambiguity of the world as something new.

For the old man, she represented something which was relevant to his own newness, to the latest, and least expected, chapter in the story of his own self-development. Dorothea was the image of the possibilities of every human life, the possibilities that had once been his.

'I was brought up as a Catholic,' Dorothea said, 'in Catholic schools. But there is something I object to in the Christian religion.'

Dorothea's newness included an absence of

reticence that was nowadays the hallmark of the young.

'How is it,' she continued, 'that a religion centred on the idea of love should have its roots in a judicial murder?'

'You mean the story of Christ's suffering and death?' the Cardinal said.

'I can understand God choosing to take on human nature for a while,' Dorothea said, 'to remind us that we're not wholly bad – to remind us that we have some sort of god-like potentiality within us – but then to leave this world as a victim! – and a bleeding victim at that! Crucifixions were a normal thing two thousand years ago, weren't they?'

'Yes. And there have always been unjust trials and executions. The medieval imagination made it into a bit too much of a horror story. And made too much of the role of the Jewish leaders. It offends our more sensitive modern imagination and our greater knowledge. But, in old age, I dare to say there is something in our traditional faith that also troubles me. We have never really solved the problem of evil.'

'Without evil there would be no need of Christianity or the Church! You have a vested interest in evil, surely.'

'You know that St Augustine had a major effect on Christian faith in its early days, and again at the time of the Protestant Reformation.'

'I know he was big on Original Sin and on sins of the flesh, including his own flesh.'

'It's only recently that I have dared to think this, let alone say it, as I am going to say it to you now, dear Dorothea. The problem is that Augustine read the book of *Genesis* literally, rather than allegorically or as a myth. And he forgot the Platonism that led him to reject Manichaeism and become a Catholic.'

'In *Genesis* it says that God saw that the world was good. And then, ten minutes later and in most of the Old Testament, it's all lust and lying and murder and mayhem. At least the Greek gods enjoyed doing their dirty deeds.'

'But wasn't it prophetic, as things have turned out?' the Cardinal said. 'There has been a great deal of murder and mayhem and lust and lying, as you call it – an awful lot of sin, to use the traditional word.'

'But do you get people to stop sinning by getting them to wallow in the story of other people's sins? It's a sort of sado-masochistic perversion.'

'The meaning of the death of Christ is his victory over evil, in an ecstasy of *love* for the human race. He didn't see us as doomed to do evil, but as fully capable of overcoming evil by struggling to be good and to do good in every moment of our lives. We call it the effort to lead a holy life. We can choose to do the will of God because that is what God loves us for doing. And sometimes we fail, and that is sin. In recent years I've prayed for a new Reformation, to rescue a human race that is more than ever in desperate need of it.'

'Some people would say that Christianity is in terminal decline, wouldn't they? Especially in Europe. People are into meism rather than theism.'

'For a while after the Renaissance privileged people believed in the sovereign individual and an idealist humanism inspired by Plato. And then, for a while after the Reformation, some Christians went back to Augustine and the lonely responsibility of the human being in the presence of a judging God. But, in the meantime, the individual human being has been consumed by the self-obsessed leviathan of the modern state. The human being is withering away.'

'Hard to imagine states being good and doing good!'

'That is the question, Dorothea. How can we reconcile the idea of the redeeming power of love with the fact of the overwhelming power of societies? I see now that that is the great challenge of the twenty-first century. Can being good and doing good be the ideal not just for human beings but also for human societies, for all humanity?'

'A holy society sounds about as unlikely as a green rose or fire in ice.'

'It may be too late, or it may not be too late, to redeem society, dear Dorothea, by redeeming religion. I see now that the Roman Church should have responded to the Reformation by going back to its roots as an ideal humanism with a superhuman dimension, a Christian religion of love and hope and joy.'

'That would be my religion!' Dorothea said. 'Optimistic and cheerful.'

A very old Catholic, the Cardinal was familiar with the reasonable confusion and doubt of any true believer. But, as old people worry about sliding into what is known as senile dementia, he worried about sliding into a state of mind in which doubt may end as despair, a dark night that may include no promise of a meeting with God, no new dawn.

A solitary cormorant was standing, its wings spread wide, staring at the interesting couple sitting on a stone bench – very old man and very young woman. Birds are human watchers as much as humans are bird watchers. Not having read the *Book of Genesis*, the bird had no reason to think anything but the best of either of them.

MORAL
*We will all meet our
Maker in a state of doubt.*

* * *

Thirteen

THE ENGLISH MEN'S TALE

A WELL-ORDERED LIFE
Talking as a way of being

'Who was Silvia? What was Silvia? Hecuba to you, you to Hecuba?

'She was my all, my everything. She came, I saw…'

'You conquered?'

'I was a puppet on her string. Putty in her hands. My angel from the far North.'

'At long last love.'

'It didn't last. She was a fallen angel. She cast me off like old socks.'

'Love's labour lost? I met a girl called Maria.'

'As in Maria, MARIA? How do you solve a problem like Maria?'

'She floated in on gossamer wings. She stole my heart. And left it in the Bronx.'

'Ah, New York. New York. A wonderful town.'

'She'd met a man from Ipanema. And that was that. I couldn't give a damn. Smiling at grief.'

'We dream.'

'There's the rub.'

'We can't complain. Swings and arrows. Ups and downs. The thick and the thin. You take what you're given. The will of God, as you might say, even if you're not specially religious.'

'Human life is a endless game of chess or snooker. You've got to think several moves ahead.'

'We are what we eat. We chew the cud, with a nice beer. Shoot the breeze.'

'Masters of our fortune. Monarch of all we survey.'

'As if.'

Conversation among English men is golf by other means. An all-weather sport. But not an amateur sport. It is a way for men to co-exist, to assert themselves in the absence of children and women. Its sanctuary is the pub or the club or the nineteenth hole on the golf course. It is a performance art, in which speaking is what counts, not what you say. Its basic raw material is what has been said before countless times by everybody.

Women talk from the heart. Normal English men talk with as little feeling as possible. Too much feeling is not good for friendly human relations.

We should not be too quick to disdain this functional use of conversation. It may be a sophisticated product of human social evolution, a response to the ultimate human challenge of living together from day to day. The brain of the human species produced language, and language made possible social life and ever greater social complexity, so that the pressure of society became an almost unbearable burden on normal human beings.

But, like all other animals, the human animal's life is lived in the most micro form, from moment to moment, day after day. The minimal sociability of unthreatening conversation may be an evolved existential necessity.

Frank Price and Ernie Wilde were better than average pupils at better than average state schools in different parts of the country. They didn't go to university. In their day, going to a university was the exception rather than the rule that it has become. They have carried their secondary education through their lives lightly, as you can tell from their conversation.

On leaving school at the age of eighteen, they had no difficulty in getting a job. They set off on a path (a rut, as they would say) towards middle management with no unreasonable ambitions. A good salary increasing gradually in a well-established firm, whose ownership was not changing every five minutes, as would be the case today. The prospect of a company pension to which they contributed.

The period from the 1960's to the 1980's seems now like a golden age for the British middle-middle-class. Compared with what their parents went through in the economic chaos of the 1930's and the war and the post-war. Compared with what their successors are going through now.

A sensible marriage, a decent enough house in a decent suburb. Good schools for their children, with an afternoon of sport and plenty of spare-time activities and hobbies. TV and radio and the newspapers and films and the pubs and football and cricket were at their best, bringing the nation together. You complained about the government because the people have always complained about their governments. But government was serious and honest then.

There was a lot to talk about as neighbours or

in the office, bringing people together, compared with the isolation and the conflictual populism of today. Conversation was an integral part of a way of being.

Frank and Ernie have always loved to talk. As senior citizens, they are still great talkers, and conscious of it. They had met each other when they came to live nearby in one of those decent suburbs and as fellow members of the local Neighbourhood Watch scheme.

Over the long years of their friendship, they had delighted in taking conversation to its limit, as a pointless but creative way of passing the time. They know that cliché and nonsense and humour are the spice of good conversation. The bland leading the bland. A British way of keeping the awfulness of real life at a safe distance for a while.

As we have heard in their improbable conversation on the subject, their love-life has not been a very big part of their lives. They are happily married, as people say about their marriage, knowing that people will understand that they don't mean it literally.

They think they are much the same as most men, who believe that random sex is for other people, especially so-called celebrities, which gives you something to talk about, in a detached moralising sort of way. And it gives you someone to pity. Celebrities and rich people in general are not happy, by definition, are they? Dating as a social activity is an American invention.

Then there is politics. Conversation is talking with no ulterior purpose. Politics is talking with a purpose. Its purpose is to take power over other people's lives. Disdain for politics as a circus is an ideal topic of everyday conversation.

'Half of them have never had a proper job in their lives.'

'They're glorified salesmen, selling themselves, to get our votes and a cushy life.'

'At our expense. We're milch cows of the public purse.'

'They are modern pharisees, Frank. Whited sepulchres. Saying this and doing that.'

'You can smile and smile, Ernie, and be a villain.'

'I don't know how they've got the nerve. How can they sleep at night?'

'Feathering their nest while they do the dirty.'

'They always say that claptrap about going into politics to do good and make the world a better place.'

'They certainly do that. Their good, their world.'

'They get away with it, Frank. Blue murder.'

'Half of them are closet Marxists. The rest are closet fascists.'

'My better half always spoils her ballot paper. I always vote Labour, without giving it much thought. They're supposed to be on the side of the people.'

'Tell that to the marines, Ernie! The people, my foot! Pull the other one. It's got bells on it. I always vote Conservative, giving it no thought at all. It's the right thing to do for property-owning citizens.'

'I'm from the north, where people are warm and sharing and caring. You're from the south, Frank, where people are cold and neurotic and narrow-minded. You're God's own Conservative.'

'I voted for bloody Brexit, Ernie. You didn't. Now I'm not so sure. Get back our sovereignty. No more Brussels bureaucracy. No more mongrel collections of slimy foreigners giving us orders. Close the gates. Independence. Britannia rules the waves. Britons shall never be slaves.'

'It was corrupt party politics, Frank. The Tories risked the future of the country to win an election. They didn't believe in it themselves. They could do the same thing with Scotland.'

'I was taken in, Ernie. We seem to be alone in the world now, with no power at all, under the thumb of foreigners, and not just Brussels. China and America. No more waves to rule.'

'Who's going to pick the fruit and serve in restaurants? Who's going to be the doctors and nurses?'

'The problem is we've never really liked foreigners. We're different, Ernie. Always have been, always will be. It's in our genes. We stumble along. We get through. The English race. God put the French and the Germans there to show us who we are. To show them who we are. And we've still got our friends across the pond. They're our blood brothers.'

'Frank, really! They're mostly former slaves and people speaking Spanish. The non-Anglo-Saxons will soon be the majority. Huddled masses and refuse from our teeming shores. Not our kith and kin. You saw that programme. They've heard of New England. But that's about it.'

'They loved Princess Di, the people's princess. And the Beatles. And Her Majesty. And Scotch. And they came to our rescue in two world wars.'

'Only after stopping to have a good think

first. There are more Germans than Brits in America, you know. You saw that programme. They rule the waves. Or did. There's China now The Chinese are much cleverer than us, Frank, than the Americans too.'

'It's just a pity the Chinese seem to want to take over the world. That can only end badly. The war to end all wars, and end human civilisation in the process, probably. Some people may not want to be taken over.'

'The Chinese are clever enough to see that for themselves, Frank. There's no point in ruling a desert. Basically, they're as sensible as us British. Practical people, like us. With an aspiring middle-class. All good societies are ruled by an aspiring middle-class.'

'Ernie, d'you know what? I sometimes wonder if you've been a closet Marxist all along. I'm not a mind-reader, but sill waters run deep, and most of an iceberg is below the surface. Remember the Titanic.'

'At least you'd be singing Land of Hope and Glory, Frank, as we went down.'

'Land of cricket on the village-green and Newcastle Brown and common sense.'

'Land of curry tikka masala and burgers and cava.'

'Land of the free and home of the brave. You lefties want to get us back to British Restaurants, like in the War, and coupons, and British Railways. They're the road to ruin. The Americans thought socialism was another name for communism, and that was that. Is it because you're from the north?'

'What's that got to do with anything?'

'You're anti London and anti the Home Counties. In your heart of hearts.'

'I sometimes wonder if it's you who's a traitor to your class, Frank.'

'What class is that, may I ask? Anyway, the class-system's a thing of the past. We're all one now.'

'No, we're not. You made it to the middle class by your own efforts and your job in the bank. The middle-class demand social change to protect their interests. The biggest thing in our lives is our family, and good family life needs a good society. Keeping up with the Joneses who want just the same thing.'

'We kick away the ladder of the past, Ernie, except for decorative purposes. Farrow and Ball and Cotswold cottages and all that. But you're right. I may be an eighteenth-century Whig at heart.'

'A Whig without the port and the gout.'

'You're really a conservative too, Ernie, in your heart. With a small "c". It's applied common sense. Using the best of the past to steer us safely through troubled waters to a new promised land over the horizon.'

'We've done alright, Frank.'

'We've done alright, Ernie.'

We who hear Frank and Ernie talking can surely feel some pride in the fact that conversation that avoids coming to blows, and may be forgotten five minutes later, was once possible, and is no longer normal in a Twittering world.

'A promised land flowing with milk and honey, it is not, Frank. Twitter is flowing with gall and brimstone, whatever they are.'

'I sometimes think I might get back to religion. I was baptised, wasn't I?'

'I wouldn't put anything past you, Frank.'

'As the years go by, and you don't get any younger, and the children leave the nest, you can't help thinking about death, and the meaning of life.'

'Many people manage not to.'

'Why are we here?'

'Because we're not somewhere else? Because

of evolution? You've seen all those David Attenborough programmes.'

'I'm a man of purpose, Ernie. Always have been. It's common sense to say we wouldn't put so much effort into living, which is bloody hard work, if there's no purpose to it all. It'd be crazy.'

'Surviving from today to tomorrow is quite a bit of a purpose.'

'But it's a purpose without a purpose. And that's a contradiction in terms. I'm struggling here. Help me.'

'I'm sorry, Frank. But you've left me behind somewhere. You'd have to buy the whole caboodle of the Bible and church and, perish the thought, the Pope, to find a purpose for everything. Wouldn't you? You're just not the bells and incense type. You're too sensible, mostly.'

'That's not the point. What I've noticed about religious people, like our friends the Callaghans, is two things. They seem cheerful, and humble.'

'You don't think that may be the Guinness they consume. If so, you're halfway there.'

'It's as if they knew something that you and I don't know. And it's something that puts them in their place, but it's a place they're glad to be in.'

'Yes. I think I've noticed what you're saying.

And it seems to have rubbed off on the Callaghan children. They're nice and sensible in an old-fashioned way. And they do their homework and wash the dishes without complaining. That's a bit of a miracle nowadays.'

'The trouble is I may have left it all too late. And she who must be obeyed may not be too keen on her husband suddenly becoming someone who is not the man she married.'

'She might be quite glad. You never know.'

We who have been overhearing the conversation between Frank Price and Ernie Wilde may feel a twinge of embarrassment that it began to take on a rather intimate aspect. And Frank and Ernie, as good Englishmen, may themselves have felt a twinge or two of embarrassment also.

'I've no idea how I could progress the religion thing. Or should I simply forget it and be sensible, like you say?'

'Why not mention it to Pru? Your wife is a sensible person, and, heaven knows, a good listener. Or you could try to get to know the Callaghans a bit better. See what makes them tick. Or you might talk to the vicar here. You met him at my daughter Angie's wedding. He seems like a sensible person.'

'Too sensible, Ernie. I need to challenge and be challenged. The Church of England is too nice.'

'I somehow feel you wouldn't want to use the direct approach and talk to a Catholic priest.'

'Theology and all that would get me nervous. Not my sort of bag.'

'The theology is apparently a bit of a thing on the side for most Catholics. Their big thing now is how to be a good human being and to do good. You saw that programme about a monastery.'

'Silence certainly isn't my big thing.'

'A monastery is the last place on Earth where you could survive.'

'You never know, Ernie. Life throws up surprises. The show must go on. Tomorrow is another day, as the bishop didn't say to the actress.'

Well-conditioned Englishmen have efficient ways of defusing embarrassment. Humour exists mainly for that very purpose.

'*Che sara sara*, Frank. As the actress said to the bishop, in his disappointment.'

MORAL
If only common sense ruled the world!

* * *

Fourteen

THE DIPLOMATS' TALE

UNCLE 12
Rebellion in the diplomatic ranks

Everyone agreed that it had been a good idea to hold the meeting in London. It was like going to heaven for a few days. Not Dante's *Paradiso*, thank God. A thousand restaurants and bars within walking distance of the Conference Centre.

Most of them affordable on the wages and expenses of international civil servants. Many of them affordable on the wages and expenses of delegates from PEASE countries. (French acronym. *Pays en voie d'avance sociale et économique.* Formerly known as Developing Countries or Third World countries.)

And the natives spoke English, some of them as a second language, especially in restaurants and bars. But you could understand them. More cinemas and theatres and clubs than you could shake a stick at, as first-language English speakers mysteriously say.

It is an important part of the work of any conference that it gives opportunities for the exchange of idea and opinions in the interstices of the formal programme, exchanges of ideas that could be prolonged in restaurants and bars, and even in hotel rooms.

There cannot be a single reader of the present lines who has not attended a conference or, at the very least, a training-course. Getting away from the family for a week, staying in hotels you couldn't normally afford, with plenty of opportunities for curricular and extra-curricular exchanges of ideas and opinions. It's its own civilising mission, in principle.

And the civilising mission is obviously very much greater when your conference is engaged in the business of Human Progress. Devolution and Redistribution are powerful words in anyone's vocabulary, but especially in the vocabulary of a UN conference. Or in the vocabulary of *The Guardian* newspaper or American Public Broadcasting.

Banging of the gavel.

'I call to order the twelfth biennial meeting

of the United Nations Committee on Local Enterprise.'

The calling to order was done by Joya Patel, formidable Indian minister who manages to combine the charisma of authority with a sense of humour, an embodiment of soft power within a carapace of hard power. Her friends call her Joy. Not something there is much of in public life in general, or the world of the United Nations in particular.

'Dear friends and colleagues, it gives me great pleasure to ask His Excellency the Secretary-General of the United Nations to address us. Mr Secretary-General, please.'

'Thank you, Madam President. Your Royal Highness, your excellencies, friends, and colleagues, ladies and gentlemen, we live in troubled times. Climate change, plagues, war and new forms of war, civil strife, failed states, ethnic cleansing, persistent poverty, mass migration, and every degree of the exploitation and oppression of human beings. You may say that human history has always been like that. So, what is new?

'Politicians and governments alone cannot solve the problems of the world, many of which they themselves are responsible for... The time has come for a Great Reversal of Roles. Top-down can no longer be the only way the world is organised. We must harness the energies, the hopes and the aspirations of the people and the peoples of the world. In the end, and in the final analysis, it is the people whom we are here to serve.'

A generic woman spoke, and a generic young person. No self-respecting international conference can begin without hearing from a woman and a young person. And preferably also, from a generic indigenous minority person.

Then it was time for a coffee-break. There was lively talk warmed by the Feel-Good Factor to which the participants felt entitled, as actors in the business of Human Progress. The fact that they were in lovely London because their job required them to be there is simply a collateral benefit of their otherwise tedious job. Yet another conference. The mass migrating of civil servants and diplomats around the world. Here one week, there next week.

After the coffee-break, the conference broke up into working-groups dealing with specific problems relating to the Great Reversal of Roles.

This meant that delegates could wander from room to room, seeking the most promising topic, with nobody able to know where, if anywhere, they were. It was an opportunity for one or two delegates to slip away from the Queen Elizabeth Conference Centre, placing their conference lanyards into their purse or pocket.

Outside the building there were people carrying placards of a distinctly undiplomatic kind. There was even some shouting. *Robbers. Parasites. Warmongers. Polluters.* And much more of that kind of thing. The escaping delegates had to be careful to avoid being on the British TV evening news or, God forbid, CNN.

That evening, in the conference hotel, something happened that is not par for the course at UN meetings. To call it a rebellion in the multinational ranks would be to over-dramatize it. To call it a shared moment of truth would be rather a dull way of describing it. Better to say that it was a short burst of collective soul-searching.

It began with the first of several rounds of pre-dinner drinks in the opulent conference hotel bar.

'We're a set of wretched hypocritical shits,' someone said. An American presumably. 'We are living and breathing liars.'

'That's what we're paid to be,' someone else said. He sounded as if he might be German.

'Come off it.' A Canadian voice. 'We speak the good conscience of our governments, who speak the good conscience of their people.'

Guffaws of laughter.

'Have you ever met a politician with any kind of conscience, good or bad?'

It was the voice of a French diplomat whose parents had emigrated to France from Senegal. Her father had been well educated there in the French fashion. She had had the best of French education in France. The French exported cynicism as part of their *mission civilisatrice*. The British exported hypocrisy. It was a sharing of civilisation, with a return on the investment of ten percent and compound interest. Civilisation, Christianity, Capitalism. The colonisers came bearing gifts. And left with them too.

'In Canada, a cloak of benevolence covers all public power, political and economic. We are blessed.'

'In Britain, a veil of ignorance covers all public power. The public temperature remains stable, with an occasional bout of fever.'

'The U.S. is a permanent state of civil war,' the American diplomat said. 'People in other countries don't realise that. And they miscalculate us. International meetings are a rest-cure for us. The taxpayers of the world, who pay for all this, know nothing about our valiant labours on their behalf.'

A sweeping gesture, apparently summoning the opulence of the hotel as a witness for the prosecution.

'Governments are like averagely unintelligent human beings,' the French diplomat said. 'Except when they have a leader who is feeble-minded or who has a perverted intelligence or who has uncontrollable instincts or who is a psychopath. That is why there are so many wars. A completely rational government is a contradiction in terms.'

'You could also be describing the ordinary sinner,' the German said. 'A completely rational human being is a contradiction in terms.'

'A good human being is not a contradiction in terms,' the Canadian said. 'There are countless good human beings. I would go to the stake believing that.'

'The truth is,' the American said, 'nobody anywhere knows anything about what we are doing here. Even our home departments don't bother to read our stuff. We could, in principle, have fun, and talk nonsense.'

'What a lovely idea,' the British voice said. 'I once wrote a parody of a speech for the annual plenary session of the UN General Assembly attended by heads of state and government. You know the thing. Excoriating the crimes and follies of their enemies. Honeying the good works of themselves and their friends. But I transposed the enemies and the friends and mixed the thing up.'

'We've all longed to do that,' the German said.

'The small problem was,' the Briton continued, 'a wicked colleague put my parody speech into the Prime Minister's weekend red box of official papers. He would have spoken it to the assembled company of the biggest of big wigs in New York. No one would have batted an eyelid, since no one would be paying close attention. But it would have gone into the written record.'

At UN meetings, spoken words float in the air-conditioned air for a while. Then they evaporate into oblivion among billions of other spoken and written words preserved somewhere for an uninterested posterity.

'But I had a crisis of conscience, and I retrieved the Prime Minister's speech at the last possible moment. Someone had written the usual speech for him, very correct, and as tedious as ever.'

'I could have written that speech in my sleep,' the German said.

By the time they sat down to have dinner in the hotel restaurant, they were mellower, but also a bit more creative in their thinking.

'I've always admired dissenters,' the American said. 'The Puritans went too far. But a bit of dissent sowed the seed that became grist to the mill of social progress, mixing my metaphors only a little.'

'I've always admired Luther,' the French diplomat said, 'He blew the whistle on the whole monstrosity of Rome. He used carefully focused obscenity as a weapon of war. As if Rome could be offended. They were case-hardened by fifteen centuries of spectacular ups and downs.'

'It's a pity that revolutions make things worse than they were,' the German said. 'Everything is thrown into the air and, when it hits the ground, it's usually the same people who are in charge, but with greater legitimacy.'

'You've described the American so-called

revolution to perfection,' the American said. 'The slave-owners and the prosperous merchants continued as slave-owners and prosperous merchants, buoyed up by the myth of freedom and by their manifest destiny to eliminate the native Americans, and to rule everyone everywhere.'

(We are not giving the names of the dissenting diplomats. They are senior and responsible public officials. No names no pack drill.)

'So we all know it's hopeless,' the Canadian said. The world will always be governed by desperately imperfect people...'

'... and an international *Hofmafia* of public officials accountable to no one.' The German had completed the idea.

'As it was in the beginning,' the Briton said, 'is now, and *erit in saecula saeculorum*.'

They stared for a while into their glasses of affordable wine, as people say about houses that can be afforded by people who can afford them.

At last, the American spoke.

'I'm not so sure, you know. Maybe there is something we can do. I was at the UN Law of the Sea Conference. On our delegation, we had unofficial members who were leaders from industry and commerce, with major interests in the world's oceans. The interesting thing was that their attitude to the international system was different from the government attitude. They make long-term investments involving billions of dollars. They want an orderly rule-based world, to protect their investments. They were entirely pragmatic about what the rules should be. They saw it as a practical problem. Not a political problem.'

'I've often found the same thing,' the Briton said. 'Such people generously see us public officials as intelligent people. They pity us for having to warp our intelligence to submit to the irrationality of politics.'

'In Germany, government is closer to big business, and, indeed, to the big trade unions. I sometimes think that it makes it more difficult for us to play well in the Great Game of diplomacy, a game which it has taken you people centuries to perfect.'

'Would it be possible for people like us,' the Canadian said, 'to see if we could find common cause with the people who have the power that finally rules the world, namely, economic power?'

'In France, the people of public power work hand-in-glove with the people of economic power,' the French diplomat said. 'They were at school together and university. They meet frequently in very private *diners en ville*, and give each other the biggest jobs, and come and go between business and government. A merry-go-round of ultimate power. *La ronde.*'

'In England, we have the advantage of gentlemen's clubs in London, which are now mostly gentlewomen's clubs also. So-called top people of every kind, including people like us, can meet there discreetly. The quiet voice of economic power is one of the voices of God waiting to be heard.'

'We have the same thing as you French and Brits, in Washington and New York,' the American said. 'In their saner moments, governments do in the end listen to industry and business.'

'I think it's true in all countries,' the Briton said. 'But, in the UK, many of our top civil servants retire into the warm and profitable embrace of business and industry. For their contacts presumably. Perhaps even for their knowledge. They go native, serving the interest of their company and the collective interest of industry and commerce, rather than the national interest or the public good.'

'I'm reminded of a strange thing,' the British diplomat said tangentially. 'In England, the 1598 Poor Law Act of Parliament required every parish to appoint four Overseers of the Poor, whose job was to alleviate the terrible condition of the poor, the old and the sick. It was a very early example of social legislation, and a second example of the devolution of power to the most local level, the first having been justices of the peace. It was a public-private enterprise. It was an early example of the devolution of power and the redistribution of wealth that this wretched conference is supposed to be about.'

'That's it. I'm going to make a proposal,' the American said, his hand on his chin to indicate deep thought, an undiplomatic tone of excitement in his voice.

'I suggest that the five of us constitute ourselves, here and now, as the Preparatory Commission for Overseers of Ultimate Power. PCOUP. We will meet from time to time to organise the relationship between holders of public power who are loyal servants of politicians, like us, and the holders of the economic power that, at the end of the day, matters most.'

'President Coolidge may or may not have said that the business of America is business, but every American administration knows that in its bones. Without business there would be nothing much to govern. But it can be a fraught relationship because business and industry speak with many conflicting voices. And governments must win elections. And business has to please its investors.'

'And that's true in France,' the French diplomat said, 'and I'm sure in Germany too.'

'It certainly is,' the German said. 'But the job of government is to be a leader in the relationship, reconciling all the conflicting interests.'

'The British Empire was made by and for trade,' the British diplomat said, 'to help the seventeenth-century Balance of Payments. They were fixated on the Balance of Payments as the measure of a successful economy. The Empire grew in the eighteenth century, making industrialism and urbanisation possible. We joined the EU in 1973 to get free trade with our main trading partners, and to help to make the EU into a post-imperial great power, or to make sure that it would never become a great power, depending on your attitude to Europeanist dreams.'

'As I see it,' the German diplomat said, 'the job of PCOUP would be to oversee the relationship between business and government, as if it were a diplomatic situation. As if they can be the best of friends and the best of enemies, like states, but capable of peaceful and profitable co-existence.'

'I would see PCOUP as a form of supplementary democratising,' the Briton said. 'We would be using our knowledge of what is really going on, and our privileged contacts, to insert some mediating ideas into the operational level of the turbulent struggle that is capitalist democracy.'

'We would be acting only in the widest public interest, of course,' the Canadian said. 'There would be nothing in it for us personally.'

'Of course,' the French diplomat said, managing to put an undertone of disbelief into her spoken affirmation. French diplomacy is coldly realist about everything other than France.

'It would be in our personal interest,' the British diplomat said, 'if only to save our self-respect and sanity, so that we can be loyal servants of governments that do their best for their people, not merely for themselves.'

'And that would be best for all the people of the world,' the Canadian said. 'As a half-intended consequence.'

'We Americans have always dreamed of sharing our natural benevolence and far-sightedness with the whole world. A city on the hill. But then we wake up.'

After some further discussion over a *digestif* or two, the PCOUP proposal was agreed *nem. con.*

So, dear reader, if you have recently noticed some surprisingly rational statements and actions by governments, you are privileged to know how that improbable thing may have come about.

MORAL
The world is ruled by the few
Get to know the right few!

* * *

Fifteen

THE CONVICT'S TALE

CRIME AND PUNISHMENT
The injustice of justice

I'm in prison for a crime I didn't commit. That's not fun, I can tell you.

It was really a white-collar offence, alleged offence, but with a gun involved, liable to intimidate, as the charge-sheet said. So it's not a country-club prison. It's this hell-hole. With murderers and rapists and child molesters and so on. Sykes, Bill. 304219. Not my real name.

I'm sharing a cell with Mike, the nicest person you could imagine. He can hardly read or write. He could read enough to drive. He's a lorry-driver. He was away from home a lot. While he was away, his wife carried on with other men shamelessly, and made a fool of him. It would take a saint not to do something about it. She ended up in hospital for a few days. And now he's here for six years.

I'm here for four years, possibly closer to three, if I don't get into trouble. Which may be difficult, as there's a lot of general violence and inter-racial conflict among the prisoners, some of whom belonged to gangs on the outside. My appeal against conviction is pending. But, in the meantime, I've just got to grin and bear it, or at least to bear it.

The odd thing is I know the man who was really guilty of my crime. He's called George. We were friends. We were in the army together in Berlin and Afghanistan. He had gone into accountancy after the army. That's a polite way of putting it. He was certainly not chartered, or whatever it is. It was mostly gambling and lending money ungenerously.

He gave evidence against me under oath. I had gone with him to see some people who owed him money. He had words with them. He said I was holding a gun. He said it must have been my old army gun, unregistered. There were no bullets in it. In fact, it was his old army gun, and he was holding it.

He told the court that I had led him into a confrontation with the debtors, and he had tried to restrain me. The debtors were too ashamed to say what really happened when they gave evidence, or were they bribed? The jury discussed the matter for one hour. I was convicted.

Me lead him? My foot. We had had a great time together in Berlin. In Afghani, he loved shooting at people, mostly the natives. In self-defence, of course, for Queen and Country. But the fact is he seemed to enjoy it. I discovered an evil side to his character that I hadn't seen before.

My wife visits me, with her mother. A nice mother-in-law! But she's Irish, and the Irish have had to put up with a lot from the English, haven't they? My two children don't visit me. I don't blame them. It must be an awful thing for them, their dad in prison.

I spend time in the prison library, where there's a computer, if you can call it a library. A few random books. I pitch in with the gardening. It helps to keep you sane. I go to classes in touch-typing and knitting, just to be sociable really.

I've got to know the chaplain. Roman Catholic. He seems like a good person. I've been to Sunday Mass. I got quite emotional, hearing him say that God knows all about us, down to the smallest detail. The problem is He can't give evidence in a court of law, not even as a character witness.

In America, there are people who spend years in the hell-hole prisons there, and then someone proves that they were innocent all along. Or years and years on Death Row, till someone proves they were innocent all along. Imagine that! And. if you're a lower-class black American, you're likely to be in prison sooner or later. Land of the free and home of the brave. My foot.

I'm writing this all down. To let off steam, yes. But also, to tell people about the lives of some of their fellow human beings, whom God may not have deserted, but practically everyone else has. The mills of the law grind slowly and erratically. The same thing could happen to anyone at any time. And you are left, day after day after day, in despair, since you are the only person on Earth who knows the actual truth about the alleged crime.

Prison is a university of life. Halls of residence with all your meals provided. A cross-section of humanity living in close confinement, for several years, or for ever. Twenty-four hours is a long time. That's something else you learn. Unless you can find ways of diverting your mind, that's an awful lot of time to spend thinking.

You cannot fail to become something of an expert on the nature of the human being, the human world, the tragedy-comedy of the human condition. Good and evil. Sin and redemption.

As a self-identified outsider, I have made a point of observing the attitude of the prisoners to their own crimes and the crimes committed by other prisoners. I have been surprised to discover that there is a sort of shared hierarchy of moral judgment, to put it rather grandly. They have different attitude to crimes of killing, crimes against property, and other crimes against the person.

Take the case of Jack, for example (not his real name). His was the ultimate case of premediated murder, what the Americans call First Degree Murder. He had poisoned his wife by small doses of undetectable poison over a period of time, a poison that, unfortunately for him, had become detectable in the meantime.

They had married at a young age, and, in middle age, he had become rich and successful and even famous. He felt the need for a trophy wife to match his new situation. She refused a divorce and had started legal proceedings to get custody of the children on the grounds of his alleged addiction to drink and drugs.

The general view seemed to be that his crime was understandable.

Or take the case of Jim (not his real name). His was a case of what the French call a *crime passionnel.* No premeditation. He surprised his wife and a man in the middle of the act, with the couple's children downstairs eating their supper. In France and Italy, the courts take a lenient view of murder in such a case. And so did Jim's fellow prisoners.

Or the cases of Arthur and Andy (not their real names) whose offences were manslaughter, respectively in a car accident and under the influence of drink or drugs. The other prisoners mostly took a-there-but-the-grace-of God view of those offences.

Or the cases of Bashir and Eamon (not their real names) who had killed people in the course of what the law calls terrorist acts. The other prisoners were impressed by the rather incomprehensible fact that they had done their offences for no personal profit of any kind, but for a cause which was bigger than them. Can there really be people like that? Isn't there something almost admirable about that?

I've been very struck by the general opinion of the prisoners about offences against property, including fraud of every kind, robbery, theft, and malicious damage to property, to use the proper legal term.

They might not know that someone had said that property is theft. They might not know that it's only the law that makes property into a sort of monopoly over the possession and use of bits of the physical world. They might not know the perfectly respectable view that justice requires that economic inequality in society should be corrected by the redistribution of wealth.

They surely don't know about utilitarianism, but they seem to know instinctively think that the job of the criminal law should be to balance the cost and the benefit to the human happiness of all those involved in the offence, offender and victim, and hence the cost and the benefit to society. Moralising prejudice is not a proper way to run a society based on property.

As to prisoners who had committed offences against the person, the other prisoners were as moralistic as anyone else. But what has surprised me is that they carefully discriminate in terms of the details of each case, like the discerning of Jesuit moral theologians.

Offences against children were unforgivable but, even there, they recognise that the offenders were addicted, and nothing was likely ever to cure their addiction, certainly not prison. And why did people allow them to go on doing what they were doing, year after year. And why did people keep re-employing them? Other people share the blame for their awful acts.

Similarly with domestic violence. If you had to live in a slum or a two-room flat with screaming children, with drink as the only escape from reality, wouldn't you have a breaking-point, as a wife or husband, an end of your tether? Mightn't you blow a fuse eventually?

And then there were cases like Les and Franco (not their real names) who were members of gangs. For a senior member like Les, guns were everyday items of clothing, like a suit for the middle-classes. For a young member like Franco, the same was true of short-bladed knives.

The other prisoners, who were not members of a gang, thank God and good luck, couldn't see how Les and Franco could escape from the only world that they know.

I hope people will not think that I am defending crime and criminals. Knowing that I am not myself a criminal, I don't have a sense of fellow-feeling with convicted criminals. On the contrary, as a responsible member of society, I must be a firm supporter of law and order and justice.

But I now see that it doesn't follow that I must support the present organisation of law and order and justice, which we have inherited from a very different past, a past that was dominated by the ideas and interests of the haves in society, who cared little or nothing about the ideas and interests of the have-nots.

I don't necessarily approve of what the other prisoners have done, any more than you don't necessarily approve of all that your colleagues at work do, or the other members of your cricket club or your political party. You pick and choose who and what to admire in this world. That is a fundamental right and freedom which is not mentioned in the pompous and dishonest and grossly unrealistic public declarations of such things.

Des, a rather incompetent burglar and repeat-offender, said something that I heard others of the prisoners say.

'School was a waste of time. If they'd taught me a decent trade, I'd have stayed in school, and none of this would have happened.'

What I have come to admire during my own current false imprisonment is a great human truth that my fellow prisoners have discovered in their imprisonment, in many cases their multiple imprisonments.

They know something, and who can have the nerve to doubt the authority of their hard-earned knowledge?

They simply know, as certainly as you can know anything, that there was no sense in the corralling of all offenders of all kinds into the same dreadful place that is a prison, like throwing all household waste into the black refuse bin.

The price to pay for the different kinds of attack on society is that each and every one of them is torn from their family, where they may be the breadwinner and where their children need them, so that their family and their children pay a great price also. And to the measured period of the removal of their physical freedom is added an ummeasured daily sentence of humiliation, indignity, loneliness, squalor, violence, insecurity, and despair. In Scandinavia they have removed that additional penalty.

The only justification offered to them is that this is how things always have been. But everyone knows that this is no longer a possible justification for standing in the way of human progress. Progress takes hold of many bad things that had existed for ever in human society and eradicates them, replacing them with better things to create new and better conditions of human social life. Re-humanising human beings after long centuries of dehumanising. But not prisons.

We don't torture suspects any longer. We don't hang, draw and quarter people who have fallen foul of the powers-that-be. We don't burn people at the stake. We don't stage public executions. We don't make children clean chimneys. We don't make workers work twelve hours a day, six days a week.

We don't flog sailors fed on rotting bully beef and riddled with scurvy. We don't leave people with mental health problems to waste away in asylums. We don't leave people to die from life-threatening diseases caused by the conditions of their work. We seek to prevent and treat every disease. We all have access to a doctor. We all have some education, and opportunities to make a better life. And many, many more.

The reader may not believe me, but I promise that I have heard all these points made by my fellow prisoners, if not so eloquently as

I have expressed them here, in their disjointed conversations, in the times when they are allowed to be together.

And they are all painfully aware of a further very real source of their despair, beyond the tragic anachronism of the prison system itself.

What is the point of a system which sends convicts back into society unchanged, with a sense of shame, with a bitter sense of injustice, and of inequality based on social class, facing the prospect of long-term unemployment and, above all, with little or no hope, in many cases, that they will not return to prison in the future? Prison can then become a default way of life.

And all this at enormous and increasing expense to the taxpayer. And yet taxpayers, other than those of the hanging, flogging, and castrating tendency, rarely give a moment's thought to what is happening in their midst, unless and until it affects a member of their own family, as it has affected me and my family.

But I will never cease to think about it. That is a promise I make to the prisoners I came to know as friends.

MORAL
Social deprivation is a life sentence.

Bill's conviction was quashed by the Court of Appeal. He is a free man, who will never feel safe again. He is a different man. His wife and children still love him. He goes to church on Sunday. He visits George in prison.

* * *

Sixteen

THE ANXIOUS THINKER'S TALE

WHEN IGORANCE IS BLISS
'Tis still necessary to be wise

I had decided to do some anthropology, sociology, scientific research, market research, whatever one might choose to call it.

I made grant applications to the usual suspects. The Social Science Research Council. The British Academy. The Ford Foundation. The MacArthur Foundation. The Bill and Melinda Gates Foundation. The Prince's Trust.

Their general view was that my project was not well focused, and too cheap. I should have applied for two research assistants and rental office space, with cost-estimates for field work.

The Beginning of the End of Knowledge. That seemed to me to be well-focused enough to be worth looking into.

As regards field work, admittedly it was not to be in the jungles of Sumatra or lost tribes in the Amazon rain forests. And it might be possible to save money by combining research work with holidays in some pleasant places in very civilised countries, where the main problem lies.

It didn't help that I am not an academic, not in university employment. I am a retired medical doctor. Dr Steve Ruskin GP. That was me. I was a GP for many years in Liverpool, and for many years in Harrogate. I am a natural people-watcher. A human entomologist, you might say. But I admit the range of conversation with one's patients was rather limited. They were often quite talkative in Liverpool, many of them of Irish ancestry. They were more buttoned-up in Harrogate.

My parents were talkative people. A tax inspector and a head teacher. My two siblings have always talked a lot. My sister went into the Board of Trade, as it was then called. Heaven knows what it's called now. Ministry of Industrial Extinction and Brexit Reality, perhaps. My brother became a Professor of History in Cambridge. They have both met many people from many countries in their work. They too are human entomologists in their own way. I am using them as a valuable source.

Since retirement I have become a bit of a jobbing writer, sometimes paid by the word for articles in newspapers and magazines. I published a book on the South Sea Bubble, which was, I think, well received. I wrote the script for a TV documentary called War Crimes in Peace Time. It was shown in German and French on the ARTE TV channel, and was, I gather, well received.

The grant applications asked me to state my Official Position. I first thought of saying Conservative of the Old-fashioned Kind. In the end I said Intellectual. In the past, until a century ago, that would have been thought to be a respectable profession.

My ARTE programme led to an invitation to give a lunch-time lecture at the Royal Institute of International Affairs in London. It was well attended and well listened-to, I think.

That, in turn, led to invitations to speak at Sandhurst Military Academy and the Civil Service Staff College. On both those occasions, I remember being somewhat troubled by the atmosphere in the Q and A period. There seemed to be a feeling that war crimes in peace time might not be an entirely bad thing.

You may ask whether I approached my new

project with prejudices. If you mean prejudices in the etymological sense, having made my judgments in advance, then, on the contrary, I am constantly shocked by what I discover. If you mean prejudices in the sense of having some ideas about what is good and what is bad in the human condition, then I must plead guilty. The survival of knowledge as an integral part of the common good is precious to me.

You may reasonably ask what I mean by knowledge. There's the rub. The whole problem may centre on the loss of one of the word's traditional meanings. Obviously, knowledge includes knowledge of facts, knowledge of specialist subjects.

But that would be classed nowadays as what is called information. And information is now the stuff of Information Technology (IT), of which the human mind is now seen as a peculiar adjunct. IT processes information, and that is what the human mind used to do. The human mind used to process information and, in the most important meaning of the word knowledge, knowledge was the product of that process. The human brain was a computer, more subtle and creative than any electronic computer, and so was its knowledge.

Also difficult to believe nowadays, the main purpose of education was to communicate information, but also to teach how to process information to produce knowledge, and to share with the student such knowledge inherited from the past, recent and ancient. Those were the days!

Notwithstanding the absence of a grant, I have tried to be methodical in my research. I've made a point of talking to many people, listening closely, making notes. I'm not in same league as the great folksong collectors, like Cecil Sharp or Bela Bartok or Anne and Frank Warner, making recordings of people singing the songs. But I'm sure I have obtained enough reliable information about people's attitudes to allow me to process it into good knowledge.

With most people, other than London black-cab drivers and conspiracy-theorists and French and American right-wingers, you've got to read between the lines of their words. I will share with you some of my hard-earned knowledge of what is going on, where possible using the very words spoken by some representative person among those whom I have, as it were, interviewed.

'Young people know nothing any longer.'

'Education is patriarchal oppression.'

'Who needs books when you've got the Internet?'

'The job of the BBC or PBS, if they've got a job, is to entertain, not to be the voice of a self-appointed liberal elite.'

'Culture is like croquet, a quaint survival.'

'High culture is the worship of dead white males.'

'Who needs foreign languages? Foreigners have nothing to teach us. Most of them speak English anyway.'

'Everyone has the right to express their view. No one is entitled to censor anyone else.'

'No one has the right to offend minorities, and they must expect what they get, if they do.'

'Hate speech is in the eye of the beholder.'

'Politicians are only in it for what they can get out of it.'

'The so-called law courts are politics by other means.'

'So-called experts think they know everything, and they know nothing.'

'The law is made by the haves to screw the have-nots.'

'Immigrants should stay where they're from, or else go back there right now.'

'Immigrants should assimilate British values or expect the consequences.'

'Money doesn't buy you happiness, but it lets you buy stuff that makes other people wish that they were you.'

'No one needs to be poor. From every log-cabin there is a road to the White House. All you need is some get-up-and-go and a bit of luck.'

'Rich people are moral success-stories.'

'It's not the job of government to pay people not to work.'

'Health and safety is political correctness gone mad.'

'Wokery is political correctness gone mad. You'll be slaughtered if you even think anything controversial any longer.'

'Greed is good, if it pays well.'

'Climate change is a self-interested myth of capitalism.'

'Property is theft. Inherited wealth is receiving stolen property.'

'Property is a fundamental human right. Inequality is natural. The poor will always be with us.'

'Why be ashamed of colonialism? We gave the Indians railways, didn't we?'

'Slavery was the normal thing in those days.'

'The stain of slavery is ineradicable, and we must eradicate its traces now, in statues and names and so on.'

'No one is above the law, except people who can afford the best lawyers.'

'Celebrities are celebrated for being celebrities. Nothing more. So what? Anyone can be famous.'

'We're not Europeans. We're British. And never the twain should meet.'

'The National Health Service is free for everyone, including those who are clever at tax avoidance and foreigners.'

'The voice of the people is the voice of God. God help us!'

'Democracy is a fraud. It's the worst form of government, apart from all the others, as Mr Churchill said.'

'Her Majesty is a saint and a treasure. Pity about her family.'

'Football (soccer football) and American Football and Australian Rules Football are the people's game. I love my team, like I love my country. The others are the enemy. War by other means, without the casualties, usually.'

'War is a game played by politicians. They'll never give it up.'

'You need a war from time to time to shake things up a bit and purify the race. It's a matter of biology.'

'Human beings are naturally aggressive. It's a matter of evolution.'

'Free will is a myth. We do what we are programmed to do.'

'Scientists are the saviours of humanity, except when they do humanity great harm.'

'God is dead. And none too soon.'

'I'm not religious, at least not in the institutional sense. It has sort of passed me by. Like clog-dancing or the bagpipes.'

This is only a sample of the current folkways of thought I've discovered. And I have left out the most extreme. 'The earth is flat. You can see the edge, when you go in a boat.' 'The Queen is manipulated by reptilian Archons.' 'The Pope is the illegitimate spawn of the Devil and a creature from outer space.' That sort of thing.

I have not put the opinions into any neat order, because that would suggest that there is an underlying logic to them. And yet, I have to say, they do seem to suggest some sort of chaotic worldview, a worldview that is anything but a worldview in the old sense of the word. A view of a meaningless world.

The following are some of my conclusions or, at least, inferences. Let me know what you think, dear reader, especially if you, like me, are an anxious refugee from the past.

1. The traditional political opposition between Left and Right seems to have faded away, leaving the vacant centre to be occupied by something that is certainly not Centrism. It is a sort of uber-political populism that is neither progressive nor conservative, neither revolutionary nor reactionary, but a random coagulation within a mental waste land, made by people who share only a sense of general existential dissatisfaction and a lazy fatalism.
2. Education, to avoid being offensive or discriminatory, must now steer a shaky course through this mental waste land, taking care not to use authority to impose any specific knowledge or opinions. That means that the pupils at school are losing the capacity to form their own knowledge or worthwhile opinions.
3. The same is true of the universities whose traditional task was to teach a high-level capacity to find knowledge and to form

soundly based opinions, on the rash assumption that some of the graduates might hold leading positions in society in their later lives where such a capacity would be a necessary condition of their exceptional responsibility.

4. I have to say that my impression is that the young don't resent this, at both levels of education, so that school and university can come to seem rather pleasant ways to pass one's time until you must leave the parental home and face the world. And the young do seem remarkably cheerful and healthy, despite everything, compared with the many-sided anguish suffered by former generations when we were young. They even seem to have come to terms with *Freudismus*, which troubled us so much. Perhaps they're all little post-Jungians. Other-determined is their version of inner-determined.

5. Or, perhaps, an advanced level of ignorance may be rather pleasant. The basis of a good and happy life in the waste land. W.H. Auden's Age of Anxiety replaced by an Age of Indifference. C.P. Snow's Two Cultures replaced by No

Culture. High Art in the grasping hands of Commerce and Entertainment. Just compare the BBC as it once was and the BBC as it is now. And weep.

6. Laziness has overtaken the Western world. Everything is designed to reduce as far as possible the need to make an effort beyond the effort of pressing buttons. If you can't get it by pressing a button, it's not worth having. No more marching armies or trench warfare, just pressing death-dealing buttons and cyber-attack buttons.

7. The people who are most adrift are the politicians. How can liberal democracy, which used to be a dialectic of Left and Right, continue to exist in a post-political waste land? The only answer so far found is to make politics into an alternative form of advertising or public relations, establishing the better brand, marketing the better story, to win just enough votes to win an election. Macpolitics, as people say.

8. Is it all reversible? No, of course not. It could only be reversed by the very mental capacities that it is displacing. UNLESS.

Unless there is somewhere a silent minority with enough of an old public-spirited worldview, and able to find within themselves an untapped source of collective social energy.

9. I will share with you a beautiful thought that I have had amid our desolation. Couldn't we rebrand the best of the old worldview things, and market it as if it were something entirely new? Given the passive mentality of everyone else, and their consumerist conditioning, it might appeal to them like a new I-phone or a new brand of yoghurt. We could call it Civilisation Plus, the New and Improved Way of Being Human.

Of course, it could be remarkably like an old way of being human, but minus the stigma of seeming to be an alien imposition.

Dear reader, tell me what you think.

MORAL
After mind. After politics. A brand-new us.

* * *

Seventeen

THE BANKER'S TALE

MISSING PERSON
Self-doubting

They are an archetypal couple of a rather privileged kind. Two children, a boy of thirteen, a girl of eleven. Two cars. A nice house in Chorleywood. He commutes by train to his work in a bank in the City of London. She is non-fiction editor of a medium-sized publisher in London, one of the few publishers that has not been swallowed up by a faceless conglomerate. She can work from home a good deal of the time.

They're not beach-holiday people. They go to interesting places, accompanied more or less reluctantly by the children, who would prefer to be on beaches, and who are in no doubt that interesting places are meant to be education by other means. Like learning the piano or another language, you'll be glad of it when you're older.

Or else they stay in Spanish paradors or a *gite,* to get away from it all and re-charge their batteries, as they say. They are keen Europhiles, at least in cultural terms, not so much in political terms. They drink moderately, but well. They prepare meals together. They don't do much entertaining at home. They go to work-related social events in London, and the occasional theatre or concert or exhibition.

For reasons that will become apparent, we will refer to the couple here as John and Jane Doe.

John and Jane are archetypal of their class and kind. They know it. They are content with it.

That is, until the day when John didn't come home in the evening. He had been on a two-night business trip to Berlin. He and Jane spoke on the telephone on the second evening. He said he would be back in time for dinner on the following day. He wasn't.

The following morning, Jane telephoned his office. They said he hadn't come in for work. They hadn't heard anything from him. She filed a missing person report with the local police. The police soon established that he had checked out of his hotel in Berlin and had taken his flight to London City Airport.

A dead person is more straightforward than a missing person. There's the autopsy, the funeral, the grieving, the probate of the will. When it's a missing person, the possibilities are endless. In the first place, is it voluntary or involuntary?

If it's voluntary, there must be reasons. The police worked through the familiar reasons. Marital breakdown, escaping creditors, escaping prosecution, escaping military service, refuge from criminals or stalkers or other people's aggrieved husbands, escape to dissipation in metropolitan fleshpots or to a life of crime, freeing yourself so you can substitute another woman for your wife, and so on and on. It seemed that none of those things applied here.

If it was involuntary, the possibilities were not good to think about, including kidnapping, risk to life and limb, terminal missing, including death.

Then, two weeks later, John Doe came home. The door-ball rang and there he was, looking haggard and dishevelled, hardly recognisable. He had a shower. They had dinner. He slept in a spare bedroom. He told Jane that he had had some sort of stroke and had lost his memory.

However, there seemed to be something beyond the loss of memory that didn't seem right. That's how Jane would explain it later. Something didn't seem right.

At first, Jane couldn't quite put her finger on that something. Then, as by a miracle, she was able to see that it was not merely something. Everything was not right.

Her own John Doe had a unique physical peculiarity on his body, which we will not be specific about here. It had been an aspect of intimacy in their relationship. Jane happened to see the pseudo-John when he was drying himself after the shower. She had noticed that he lacked that physical peculiarity. She told the police.

They arrested him. DNA from a hairbrush belonging to the real John Doe settled the matter beyond doubt. The police intensified their investigations. They worked very thoroughly and very fast. But, if John's life is to be saved, it will not have been by their efforts alone, but because of the attention to detail of his own dear wife.

During their investigation at John's place of work, the police uncovered an ambiguous skeleton in his cupboard. It seems that he had been accumulating a great deal of money from an off-the-books side-line, apart from his normal work in the bank.

He and Jane had separate bank accounts. His account contained large amounts of money, accumulated over about eighteen months.

The police also discovered that he may have been intending to use some of the money, if not all of it, to buy the publishing company that Jane works for, to save it from the jaws of a conglomerate with a well-known face, which was showing an interest in the firm. Whether she would have been happy with John's plan is another matter.

The police also discovered that John Doe's extracurricular activities had attracted the interest of a criminal gang that specialises in financial crime of many different kinds. A sort of London-based mafia. It had long claimed the attention of Scotland Yard and MI5.

Had they already approached him directly? That was not clear. If so, was he co-operating with them, which might explain the great quantity of money in his personal account? He was certainly capable of helping the gang in many different ways, not least in the immensely profitable business of insider trading.

The police discovered that the gang in question had made use of an app on the Dark Web which allows you to find people who look like other people. Why anyone would want to do such a thing is, of course, a mystery to most decent people. But then, so is the whole of the Dark Web, which is the *fons et origo* of an infinite array of forms of criminal activity, which you and I only hear about occasionally when it rises to the surface of the media like a shoal of killer whales.

So, the gang had evidently found somebody who looks remarkably like John Doe. It seems that the plan was to substitute him for the real John Doe, send him to the marital home, where he would recover his memory immediately, get into a fight with his pseudo-wife as soon as possible, walk out, and abandon her. They had the real John Doe's passport. Now they would have his identity. Identity theft. That is apparently also a fairly common-place modern permutation on the inexhaustible possibilities of crime.

The idea was to place the false John Doe in the bank, *unless,* in the meantime, the real John Doe could be persuaded into staying in the bank, while working also for the gang. He could tell the people in the bank that he had had a stroke on his return from Berlin, and he had suffered temporary memory loss. You don't have to be unreasonably cynical, dear reader, to believe that we all have our price, however decent and upright we might otherwise be.

You might think that the mafia plan was somewhat cock-eyed. But remember, in the real world, including the world of legitimate endeavour, governmental and corporate and private, cock-eyed schemes are two a penny every day of the week, often involving computers, wasting millions of pounds, and sometimes wasting human lives. And so it is also in the world of criminal endeavour.

It emerged that the gang had been keeping the real John Doe in some comfort in a mafia safe house in a place that will not be identified here. Organised crime models itself on organised government, without the complication of elections or the law of the land.

The British authorities had been watching the innocent-looking detached house for some time. They had intercepted the gang's communications, including their encrypted messages. Surprisingly, even improbably, their communications were sometimes in Italian and Russian. Organised crime has kept pace with the globalising of commerce and industry and finance, even if the globalising of government has lagged far behind.

The British authorities strongly advised the real John Doe not to reveal to anyone the precise details of his detention by the mafia gang. It could threaten some much more important long-term operations that were underway. Of course, John agreed to this without hesitation.

It had been fortunate that the pseudo-John had a shower, and that Jane had been observant, and that the police had been swift and competent in their enquiries. Who can say what might have happened otherwise? People can be caused to be missing people permanently, without very much difficulty. Who knows how close the real John Doe had been to premature termination?

So, all's well that ends well, you may be thinking. Alas, not.

John and Jane found that it was difficult to return to their devoted archetypalism in Chorleywood, as if nothing had happened. They had changed. They had become different people. And, it must be said, a partner's hidden second life, even if its intention were to be benevolent, can easily unsettle a partnership. It suggests a lack of trust, and trust is surely at the heart of a good relationship, as psychotherapists and priests will tell you. Or else you may have learned that wisdom, dear reader, from your own life-experience. One may hope not.

Their children were basking in the reflected glory of their parents' notoriety and their presence on the social media, Instagram, and suchlike. But their parents had decided to live apart, at least for a while. They were still the best of friends, as celebrities say when they are daggers drawn, to pacify their respective fans.

John's bank has kindly given him a period of gardening leave, to see whether he will be able to get back to work satisfactorily after his traumatic experiences.

And it's possible that they may be having their own look at his newly discovered extracurricular activities. It can't be excluded that they may decide that those activities could well be made intra-curricular, since they seemed to be surprisingly profitable. Money-making is to money-makers what crime is to criminals. An existential drive.

John is spending his gardening leave in exile in a nice hotel on the Lido in Venice. Not, alas, the *Grand Hôtel des Bains* of *Death in Venice* fame. It no longer exists.

Venice contains in its bones a past full of enormous ups and downs. It is like an aged *roué* who has seen everything and done everything and has no illusions left, but whose story-telling grips you. Just the job when you are thinking about the ups and downs of your own life. What if a prosperous life is not a good life for me, still less the best life? But then, what if I'm no good at anything else?

With time on his hands, John finds himself in writerly mode, like so many people in Venice before him. His thinking aloud takes the form of putting various deep thoughts on paper, such as the following.

'Life and death are mere incidentals in the important business of commerce, as in the more trivial business of sex. Doing business is an important aspect of Freud's reality principle, the ego asserting itself, and it is a natural presence in Jung's collective unconscious. Didn't Adam Smith say that the propensity to truck, barter, and exchange is inherent in human nature and, as such, it is the ultimate source of the wealth of nations?'

'We should respect the business of industry and commerce. It has made modern civilisation. It rests on three *moments,* in the sense of the word *moment* used in mechanics: a turning force. *Das Moment* as opposed to *der Moment.*

Value added and *profit margin* and *competition*. Crucial turning forces in the labour of making and selling things.'

'A world not based on making and selling and buying would not survive for five minutes. But we are not obliged to love it in all its forms and ways, some of which are immoral, some of which are illegal, and many of which are simply unpleasant.'

'But if life as we know it is not the good life, then what on earth would the good life be?'

We should hasten to explain that the John Doe's account of his recent experiences, loyally self-censored in accordance with the wishes of Her Majesty's Government, will be thoughtful, but more like a Graham Greene novel than an Open University lecture.

'For people in so-called rich countries there is a double bind. There is no half-way house between total self-surrender to the economic system and the life of a hermit. The double bind is caused by the fact that we've come to think of our comfortable life as the necessary condition of a decent life, which we would now be incapable of living without. We don't need a yacht. We do need kitchen machinery, electronic boxes of all kinds, foreign holidays and so on and on. They're necessities, not excesses.'

'Or else. PERHAPS. Maybe there is a half-way house. Hypocrisy. We could do our job normally, to pay for the necessities of life, but despising and deploring the economic system that enslaves us, despising and deploring ourselves for being enslaved. *Homo sapiens. Homo rationalis. Homo laborans. Homo hypocriticus.* The latest form of human self-evolving.'

'But the saddest thing is that we would have nothing to look forward to other than retirement, when we might finally make our dreams come true. But when, in fact, as we know perfectly well by observing others, declining income and declining energy, not to mention the withering life-force in general, mean that we would have to go on dreaming, but now with nothing at all to look forward to, except death.'

'The human condition of most people in most so-called rich countries! Triumph of umpteen thousands of years of human self-evolving!'

There was much more such profound ratiocination which the reader can well imagine, drawing on their own introspection and experience.

Even in its factually discreet form, John's story might be substantial enough to be published by Jane's firm. It could make an excellent film, with the documentary gaps filled in by the inexhaustible imagination of the screenwriters and director.

It's a story that has the merit of being about privileged people in one sense, who turn out to be ordinary people in another sense.

John already had in mind various actors who might have the honour of representing himself and Jane on the silver screen and/or Netflix.

By the way, Jane's firm has been swallowed up by the conglomerate with the well-known face which had been showing an interest in the firm. She is now a senior editor in the merged entity. She is also helping someone who is making a documentary about the use of the Dark Web in organised crime. We must hope that this is not putting her own life in danger or putting her in danger of herself becoming a missing person.

The reader will probably have sensed the following already. But we should record the fact that John and Jane Doe are as grateful for their little adventure as they are half-proud of it. When your life is in a rut, you need the adventitious help of a passing Land Rover to pull you out of it. So long as it doesn't run you over in the process.

Who can say what the future holds for them, separately or together? All we can predict with some degree of certainty is that it will probably not include domesticity in Chorleywood.

MORAL
Get some nice pastimes and hobbies,
just in case!

* * *

Eighteen

THE CONNOISSEURS' TALE

THE MYSTERY OF ART SOLVED
The last of the few

They had decided to podcast for posterity a discussion of their philosophy of the fine arts and music and literature formed from their life-time experience. They wanted to contribute something empirical to the age-old problem of explaining the overwhelming power of the best works of the human imagination. An Anatomy of Art. Doing something of what Robert Burton did so helpfully for melancholy, an equally important subject.

And they were well placed to do so. An Anglo-German couple living in London and Berlin, with the cultural richness of those two capital cities available to them. And with a well-stocked library of their own. Their house was in Primrose Hill, close to, but not in, Hampstead. This allowed them to avoid the risk of being taken for pseudo-intellectuals, if ever there could have been such a risk.

And we are privileged in that we can share in this sample of the product of their important experiment, if only as observers.

They explained that they were not average consumers of the works of the imagination. They had little or no experience of the work of the imagination at lower levels, including popular culture. Their opinions were not based on any comparison with such things. This was not intellectual snobbery on their part, nor the superciliousness of class. It was simply that such things were not, and never had been, within their shared field of vision.

'A novel is a slice of life,' Greta May said, 'But so is a daily newspaper. The good novel must be something more.'

'The daily newspaper is an accepted form of fiction,' Adam Hutton said, 'which people suppose is a slice of life.'

'A newspaper takes minutes to read, and minutes to forget. You don't forget a good novel.'

'E.M. Forster, or maybe it was F.L. Lucas, said that a novel must show the development of the main characters, reflecting the dynamic of human life.'

It was Thomas Mann's *Buddenbrooks* that had caused them to focus on novels as works of art. His book may be too much a slice of life, of bourgeois life, which is rarely interesting.

'His *Magic Mountain* is more than a slice of life,' Adam said.

'It implies ideas.' Greta said. 'I'm never quite comfortable with a novel of ideas. Proust said it was like a coat with the price-tag still on it. You make the effort to work out what the ideas are, and you wonder why they weren't put into an essay instead.'

'The extreme case is Aldous Huxley,' Adam said. 'Not *Brave New World,* the others, where the ideas are set in the amber of page after page of turgid prose.'

'Voltaire's *Candide* is a little novella about one big idea. Nobody is sure which of two ideas it is meant to be, but that doesn't stop it being a book you can never forget. The extreme case is *Tristram Shandy* or *Don Quixote* or *Finnegan's Wake*. Larger than life, and full of ideas. You don't care about the ideas, and yet the books stay in your mind for ever.'

'They're giving a new angle on life, Greta. And that is exciting.'

'An interesting case is Dickens. Even the

light-hearted ones, but also the others, are real life. Dickens creates perfect alternative realities. That is a marvellous thing of fiction at its best. Creating reality out of nothing, out of the empty air. Using nothing but words on paper.'

'And the new way of looking at everyday life takes root in the reader's mind, as if it was life the reader had personally experienced. *War and Peace* was surely meant to do that. But somehow it doesn't work for me, Greta. Beautifully written. But old-fashioned war and Russian high society may be too remote from our lives. Tolstoy added an essay giving the idea behind the book.'

'The most interesting case is Dostoevsky,' Greta said. 'His whole œuvre is a passionate story about human life in all its forms. And we *feel* his ideas in our bones, even if countless books have been written trying to say what those ideas are. Somehow his books reach right inside us, getting into our souls irresistibly.'

'Soul to soul, even if his is a rather Russian soul. And yet somehow the author is always present in your sympathy as you read it.'

'Perhaps that's because we know so much about the author's dramatic life.'

'The interesting case is Proust,' Adam said. 'He said that the reader shouldn't know anything about writers or about their life. He himself uses a distancing Narrator, but it's too obviously Proust himself, telling a story of his own life, and the life of other people whom he always sees through his own eyes. But it's a great portrait of a particular collection of human beings and a particular society at a particular time, with shamelessly intelligent discussions of almost everything on Earth along the way.'

'I'm not the world's greatest fan of Proust, as you know, Adam. The Narrator's supposed straight love-life is simply not convincing. *Recherche* is certainly full of ideas. Proust was keen on Schopenhauer and Bergson. But he really has only two big ideas. *We become what we already are. To live a good life is to tell a good story to ourselves about our becoming.*

'You and I decided long ago what the best kind of novel really is, Adam. And it's not a very complicated idea. A *good* novel is a novel that changes us as a person. A *great* novel is a novel that makes us into a more substantial human being, like a good religion.

'Great literature is a moral act, and a moralising act,' Greta said. 'Virginia Woolf can make you a more substantial human being even if you know nothing of the price that she paid for her genius in her own life.'

Greta and Adam had always taken the view that the most difficult problem in judging works of the human imagination concerns music. What is it that places music among the greatest works of the human imagination, the greatest works of art?

'The best music doesn't represent anything,' Greta said. 'It's certainly not a slice of life.'

'And we always feel a bit uncomfortable if we are told that some piece of music has a programme, even some connection to the natural world, let alone some nationalist sentiment or even a love-of-humanity sentiment.'

'*Alle Menschen werden Brüder. Seid umschlungen, Millionen! Diesen Kuß der ganzen Welt!* I'm afraid I've always felt that those sentiments are somehow out of place, however much it may thrill audiences to hear it sung with feeling. Beethoven was as serious a human being as a human being can be. He would never have wanted to please audiences for the sake of pleasing them, least of all with sentimental ideas. Schiller may have meant it sentimentally when he wrote the poem. Beethoven should have left his music to speak for itself.'

'I have something of the same feeling about Bach's *Matthew Passion*,' Adam said. 'Even non-religious people are in awe of it. But it reflects an aspect of Christianity which is a negation of the deep joy of Christianity. The ideal of Christianity is present in the other music of J.S. Bach and in Palestrina and Victoria and Mozart and Schubert and Byrd and Tallis and Handel, and so on.'

'A limiting case is Wagner,' Greta said. 'The *Gesamtkunstwerk*. The art-work encompassing all others.'

'I'm certainly not a perfect Wagnerite. The *Ring* is all about ideas and tiresome Nordic mythology. One may be embarrassed by his nationalistic ideas. Hitler wept listening to *Lohengrin*. But somehow that doesn't affect one's appreciation of the great glory of the music. It's also strange that he didn't fundamentally change the nature of the music that came after him.'

'You and I have agreed, Adam, that the secret of music in its highest manifestation is that it always feels to be something above and beyond us, something that transcends us. It is not a mirror of us, even if it becomes part of us. And we feel desperately humble in the presence of the technical skill and the creative imagination of the best composers.'

'And the superhuman skill of the best performers. The miracle is that each piece of music is new and unique, and yet we hear it within a world of the mind in which all music is present together, and which allows us to recognise the newness and originality of each piece.'

'All music is part of a single phenomenon of the phenomenal world,' Greta said, 'Entering our minds and our souls through one of the senses. Music is sounds in a particular order. It is language without words, but it shares in some underlying grammar or syntax which gives the form to all music in all cultures at all times.'

'You're beginning to go a bit Chomskyish there, Greta. You and I don't approve of his idea of postulating an *Ur*-language from which all languages are derived.'

'But the only way we know the uniqueness of a given piece of music is by placing it unconsciously in relation to all other music that we've ever known. All music is a variation on the theme of the possibilities of sound. A Schubert song and a Wolf song. A Palestrina

Mass and a Mass by J.S. Bach. A Beethoven symphony and a Mahler symphony. A Mozart opera and a Wagner opera.'

'There I agree, Greta. Wagner wouldn't have been possible without Berlioz. Berlioz wouldn't have been possible without Beethoven. Beethoven wouldn't have been possible without Haydn and Mozart.'

'At the very highest levels, music is a competition among the best composers, And the best composers are the best because they do best in competition with other composers who have faced the same challenge, and in competition with themselves.'

'There is something about string quartets that reaches a limit of the possibility of music. The timbre of the instruments in perfect consonance. A sharing of the soul of the composer with our soul through the souls of the four exceptionally sensitive people who are the performers.'

'Music at its most abstract can be at its most beautiful,' Greta said. 'I think Beethoven would like to have written Bartok's quartets, but, of course, he couldn't have done.'

'It's interesting that atonal and minimalist music have had so little effect on Western music,' Adam said. 'Adorno says that it's the alienating effect of modern society. People no longer make the effort to understand anything difficult. It seems too much like hard work.'

'He's right,' Greta said. 'It's like serious literature and the most difficult arts in general. Serious music is a victim of cultural populism and the general laziness of modern society. We connect to the world from our sofa, with a keyboard and a remote control. Grasshopper minds in a gadfly world.'

'To appreciate the greatest works of visual art certainly requires effort. All great painting or sculpture or architecture is also a variation on the rest of great painting and sculpture and architecture. The great artists of the Italian Renaissance at its peak, from 1480 to 1520, were fiercely competitive weren't they, Greta?'

'Vasari was a lesser painter, but he was already placing the best artists in a league table. And, ever since, painters and sculptors have also made their art in full consciousness of what had gone before, inspired by it and trying to surpass it. And that's why we try to learn as much as we can about the great art of other cultures.'

'We need to know what Persian and Chinese and Japanese and Moslem and pre-Columbian and African artists, and indigenous artists everywhere. We may love their art for its own sake, but, if we know about its history and its context, it gives greater depth and value to our love.'

'And the same is true of drama, surely, Adam. The three Greek tragedians set the benchmark for all subsequent drama of the highest order. The originality of the universal genius called Shakespeare lies in what he shares with them, and what he doesn't share with them.'

'And Shakespeare was presenting a slice of the life of people whom the Greek tragedians would have recognised as human beings, remarkably like their own mythological people.'

'People might think us rather odd because we worship a German verb.'

'*Aufheben.* It contains most of philosophy. It explains great art.'

'It's the dialectic from Plato to Hegel and beyond,' Greta said. 'Dialectical opposition is resolved in something that contains the opposition, negates the opposition, and surpasses the opposition. *Aufhebung*! God bless the German language.'

'The dialectical opposition among artists and composers and writers,' Adam said. 'The opposition between the work of art as a work of the imagination and the reality it represents. The opposition between the present and the past of the art and the artist. The opposition among the eyes of all the different beholders of the work over the passage of time who all see different things in it.'

'You wrote a piece for *Apollo* magazine about that, Adam. The best works of art contain all those oppositions and negate them. Ancient Egyptian art and Mesopotamian art and ancient Geek art and Hellenistic art and Roman imperial art and Christian art and High Renaissance art and Mannerist art and baroque art and rococo art and neo-classical art and impressionist art and modern art. An age-old process of incorporation and negation and surpassing.'

'I'd been reading Joshua Reynolds, Greta. He said that the great artists of the Italian Renaissance discovered the idea of *art*. Art-in-itself. *Die Kunst an sich*. They saw that artists were able to do something of immense human significance, something which was somehow of great spiritual significance. The human imagination was creating beauty, beauty that was even more beautiful than the beauty of the world made by God. They were out-doing the creative work of God.'

'Tolstoy said that the Renaissance invented Art with a capital "A" as a substitute for religion when they ceased to believe in Christianity, pretending that a pleasant pastime of the privileged classes was some superhuman thing.'

'Tolstoy was wrong about absolutely everything, Greta. He thought that human beings were unable to rise above our animal instincts and primitive feelings. Sensible people know that the highest art makes us into more valuable human beings and human societies. That's why it's a moral and moralising act.'

'Coleridge said it best, Adam. The artist puts their consciousness into the work of art. And their consciousness takes effect in our consciousness as a we look at their work. And we make it our own. It changes us.'

'The artist creates something out of nothing by allowing their imagination to act on the physical world. Paint, stone, wood, ivory, sounds, words. Magic.'

'And the deeper and wider the consciousness that is transferred the greater the work of art.'

'A transfer from the soul of the artist to the soul that appreciates the work of art. I'm a bit more of a Platonist than you, Greta.'

'You are the Plotinus of Primrose Hill, dear Adam.'

'I believe that a work of art, each to its own degree, participates in the One of truth, beauty and goodness. The Ideal. The transubstantiation of the Ideal. The real presence of the Ideal in the work of art.'

'A painting by Mantegna. A Palestrina Mass. A Bach cello sonata. A Mozart opera. A sculpture by Michelangelo. A building by Palladio.'

'A painting by Turner. A Greek tragedy. Racine's *Phèdre.* Dante's *Commedia.* Shakespeare's *Tempest.* A novel by Dostoevsky.'

'And the same is true of art from all cultures and all times, Adam, beginning with cave paintings transmitting consciousness over millennia.'

'And there is a corollary, isn't there?'

'There is a corollary, Adam. In judging the highest works of the creative imagination, one person's opinion is *not* worth as much as the opinion of any other person.'

'I once heard a professor of the history of art, a German refugee, say exactly that to an audience of young students at Stanford University. You could hear their shock, in the darkness of the lecture-theatre. Vile elitism. We will no doubt be cancelled by saying it today, crucified in the electronic public mind. Except that, no one will listen to our podcasting.'

'It would be nice to be martyrs in the apostleship of high art, Adam.'

MORAL
The soul of the few is blessed
by the art made by the very few.

* * *

Nineteen

THE RICH YOUNG MAN'S TALE

AN ACCIDENTAL HERO
In the right place at the right time

'*Lob dem Retter! David! Der Heilige!*'
'We owe our lives to this fine young man. No question.'
'*Caro Davide! Carissimo! Ci hai salvato la vita. Tu sapei?*'
'¡*Qué bravo! ¡Campeón! ¡Salvador!*'
'*La nécessité découvre l'homme. Voici l'homme à nous!*'

David Barclay was a master of his own language, but only of his own language. But he could tell from their multilingual excitement that some of those who had been with him on Mount Etna approved of his moment of instinctive leadership.

TV news channels had collated images and sounds from an assortment of cameras and cell phones to construct a mini epic out of his exploit. He himself thought of his feat as memorable rather than sensational.

The images were dramatic. Tourists, distributed like multi-coloured ants across the lava-strewn summit of Etna, were picking their way carefully across the rough surface. Excited by the proximity of danger, they were filming and photographing each other against a background of jets of steam and sprays of black lava.

Then everything changed. A rumbling roar from the bowels of the Earth. An explosion of steam and lava far into the sky. Silence. Then a much greater explosion filled the sky with hissing steam and white-hot lava. Nature, all-powerful, self-willed, and oblivious of mere human animals.

Some of the tourists were still filming and photographing. Others were shouting. Some were screaming. For good reason. Under layers of new lava, the path that had brought the visitors to the summit had disappeared. The frantic human ants stumbled erratically. There was no way down.

David Barclay, whose English weather-eye had caused him to foresee rain, waved his multi-coloured golf umbrella vigorously above his head, and heard himself shouting "Follow me!" in a voice that he hardly recognised as his own.

The motley multinational collection of terrified tourists struggled to join him, gathering into an untidy snake behind him, queuing to be saved.

As the last of them left the summit, the volcano roared once more. Vulcan's angry warning to humans who wantonly persist in invading his privacy.

Then they were safe, huddled together, releasing their emotion in vigorous talk, repeating fervent words of gratitude for their salvation. They hugged David until he ached. They made him sign his name in their guidebooks and travel journals. His inspirational image would be reverently displayed in homes from Inverness to Istanbul, from Beijing to Butte, Montana.

Twelve hours later, the memorable event had become a global sensation, Breaking News, told and retold by journalists always on the look-out for that best kind of human-interest story, with a life-threatening beginning and a life-affirming ending.

But this story was more than that. One of those whose lives David had apparently saved was not just another tourist. Hearts throbbed, social media twittered, when they heard that humanity had come close to losing one of its specially chosen ones – a bright star in the firmament of global stardom. Yusa O'Yuro. Saved! A miracle beyond miracles! All praise to the three-in-one God of sport and light entertainment and people-news!

Hearing it said, again and again, that this eruption of Etna had been the most serious in living memory, David finally accepted that the episode had been more than merely memorable.

The mass media soon find other so-called 'stories' to feed the public's insatiable appetite for what is called 'news'. Mass-produced news may be some part of some person's life-story. The news ceases to be new. Personal life goes on.

And lo! More human interest! More news! Twelve months later.

Seeking isolation, David had rented a cottage on the Welsh island of Anglesey in sight of the sea. It was a whitewashed cottage with the frames of its four windows painted apple-green, and an apple-green front-door. It was the kind of cottage that children draw, inspired by a precocious longing for security and simplicity in their fragile lives.

David soon established his morning routine. Wealthy enough not to need paid employment, he was efficient in making his own regular habits. By ten o'clock he was installed at the top of the beach of smooth sea-swept sand. Green folding chair. Two books, light-reading and heavy-reading. Watercolour-painting materials. Fruit and chocolate and bottled water. An old wooden music-stand, bought in a Camden Town flea-market, to act as an easel.

It was that perfect month of July in 20--, the month that everyone remembers. In both Earth's hemispheres, Nature seemed to smile, for a moment, on the long-suffering human race – no wars, plagues, tsunamis, floods, droughts, earthquakes, invasions, revolutions, or volcanic eruptions. For a fleeting moment, we could imagine that Nature was congratulating itself on the human race as one of its better inventions.

David swam briefly in the placid sea – very briefly, because the early-morning sea was cold. Sitting at ease in his folding chair, he let his senses go free, watching the restless edge of the sea slapping against the wet sand, snow-white clouds forming and re-forming, the sun moving lazily across the constantly changing blue tones of the sky. He made an occasional effort to catch an impression in his sketchbook of a timeless and undemanding and reassuring scene.

He watched the other people on the beach, each family a little self-contained society, more or less orderly, more or less self-absorbed. He watched one family in particular. Three children – a boy of, say, thirteen; two girls of, say, ten and eight – David's inexperienced guess. Each of the three children at a temporary peak of the perfection of youth.

On their first morning on the beach, their father organised the little family enclave in the way that fathers should – umbrella, picnic table, chairs, towels, ice box, and all the other necessities of a day on the beach. He sat for an hour or more reading newspapers, turning from time to time to talk to his wife and his children, perhaps discussing with them something in the newspapers. To David's inexperienced eye, the children seemed capable of intelligent conversation with an adult.

The father played, unenergetically, with the children – some apparently rule-free game with racket and ball. Several times he walked purposefully from the rocks at one end of the beach to the rocks at the other end, the children following erratically, merrily.

The boy would go into the sea by himself, leaving his sisters paddling at the sea's edge. He would lie on an inflated mattress, using his arms as flippers, his usual destination a spit of sand standing out above the surface of the sea. Standing on the spit of sand, he waved to his mother and his sisters, willing them to acknowledge his achievement of each small adventure.

On the family's second morning, the father was not there. The mother was in charge. David could not decide, from a distance, what sort of woman she was. She seemed to talk to the girls almost as equals, more motherly in dealing with the boy – somehow detached from all of them, as if she had other horizons in her mind. But the little group seemed to be bound together by effortless affection.

It wasn't that David envied them. Not having a family of his own, he had long since ceased to envy apparently happy families. But he admired this family for seeming to show, at least to his idealising eye, the ideal potentiality of a young family.

It is a test of a good book of a serious kind that it can fully occupy the concentrated attention of a reader who is reading it on a beach. The serious book he was reading had fully occupied David's attention for more than twenty minutes (an unusually high score). By this time in the afternoon, the tide had brought the fringe of the sea to within several metres of where he was sitting.

Now his attention was sharply diverted to what seemed to be the distant sound of a boy's voice shouting.

The boy was, indeed, shouting – and waving vigorously. The bright red inflated mattress was almost out of sight, driven by an offshore wind. The sea had covered the spit of sand. The boy was up to his ankles in the water. Between him and the beach there was now fifty metres of deep water.

The beach was almost deserted. The boy's sisters were digging in the sand. His mother was sitting in a deckchair with earphones over her ears. Her eyes may have been closed.

Peremptory duty called. David ran towards the boy's mother, waving and shouting. Then he walked into the sea and began to swim, against a current flowing round a headland. He took hold of the boy around his waist – half walking, half-swimming back to the beach.

Not a difficult rescue, but possibly a necessary rescue.

His mother was in tears and confusion. His sisters were in tears, clutching at the boy, as if it to make sure that he was still there. The boy was peculiarly cheerful. Adventures are meant to be adventurous, as any normal boy knows.

The whole episode, small in one respect and large in another, thereafter took an unfortunate turn towards the larger end of the public spectrum. Someone had called the local police, who arrived when they were no longer needed. They took notes in their notebooks. They spoke to their superiors, and to the Coast Guard.

Very soon it emerged that the children were the grandchildren of a former French President – a man whose interesting private life had been grist for the mill of people-journalism far beyond the frontiers of France. Not much thrilling of voyeuristic hearts on this occasion, but plenty of social twittering.

David was particular in *granting*, as he put it, radio and TV interviews. For TV interviews, his favour fell on an Indian TV channel, the French-language RTL, and WTNH Connecticut. The media interest was, once again, global.

'Are you a religious man, Mr Barclay?' an American reporter asked him, linking David's two apparently miraculous feats of rescue – first on Etna, and then on Anglesey.

David had expected to be asked whether he was a witch, a bringer of bad luck, cashing-in on the good luck required to undo bad luck.

'Not institutionally, no,' David replied. 'But I have a philosophy of life.'

'Could you tell us a little bit about that philosophy of life?'

'Humanity is capable of improving itself, individually and collectively, guided by ideas and ideals that are universal.'

'I see.'

The fact is that David was no more naturally inclined than any other Englishman to think philosophically, let along metaphysically. However, brushes with death, one's own or other people's, can make one think a bit more deeply. About the purpose of life, and so on. Especially when you have been reading a very serious book. A book of German philosophy, no less.

Until he answered the reporter's question, he had not known that he had a philosophy of life. Not a bad one, either. He was a congenital optimist, and, combined with more than enough personal wealth, that did make him naturally inclined to generosity towards his fellow human beings, some of whom were, as he well knew, less privileged. And all of them needed a lot of improvement.

The One, the We, the All. I, David Barclay, (a One, and probably also an Only) am part of the WE who are the human family. Together we are part of the All that includes angry mountains that may spew death and destruction to defenceless, if intruding, human beings. And the All includes the boundless Ocean of the world which, even confined within a modest bay on the island of Anglesey, can put at risk the lives of the most innocent and vulnerable of human beings. Serious thinking indeed.

David was pleased to notice that this sudden access of philosophy, of metaphysics even, seemed to be a pleasant experience, rather like eating squid for the first time. He would have to try it again.

On a visit to Paris, he was glad to be invited to a dinner at Fouquet's with the rescued boy and his sisters, who proved to be charming and sophisticated, and the boy's parents, who were gracious and touchingly grateful. Each member of the family accepted some degree of blame for what had happened.

David said that his attention had been distracted by a book he had been reading on the beach. It had been given to him as a birthday present by a rather intimidating German friend, who had evidently not spent very much time in England or with half-educated English gentlemen. Nietzsche's *Human, All Too Human*. Oddly absorbing. And it may have infected him with the bug of philosophy and metaphysics.

As a congenital realist, however, he realised that high-class philosophy, even idealist philosophy, for which his expensive public-school education had not prepared him, could be a useful addition to his general wealth. It was an invisible asset that would be immune from the vagaries of all imaginable market forces, and it would surely never cease to give a good return on the intellectual investment. It might even be marketable.

He was looking forward now, almost eagerly, to his next meeting with his intimidating German friend.

'An intellectual equal!'

MORAL
*If you go in for saving people's lives,
it may change your life.*

* * *

Twenty

THE ALIEN'S TALE

THIS ENGLAND
Dystopian utopia

Two strangers meet on a train travelling from York to London.

'Hi. I'm Jack. Jack Gaddi.'

'Hello. Nicholas Elliott. How d'you do? You're American, I think.'

'Right. And you're English, I guess.'

'What brings you to England?'

'I live here.'

'Oh, sorry.'

'Nothing to be sorry out. I'm here by my own choice and free will. I'm a writer. I could live anywhere.'

'You're famous, aren't you?'

'Have you read anything of mine?'

'Sorry, no, I must admit I haven't.'

'Lucky you. The people who read my books, millions of people, are not the sort of people I would like to know.'

'And yet you keep writing.'

'It's a sort of prostitution. Very profitable, I can tell you. It seems crazy you can make millions from making things up for a couple of months.'

'Some people make millions in less than a second by pressing a button.'

'Crazy. What do you do for a living?'

'I'm a civil servant. Home Office, in London. I was just visiting my very elderly parents in York. May I ask why you're living in England?'

'Two reasons. To escape from the United States. And because I love England.'

'England is rather small beer compared with the United States, isn't it?'

'A little island detached from the Eurasian continent by twenty miles.'

'Several thousand islands actually.'

'That's part of the charm, Nicholas. No one knows what England is.'

'The Welsh, the Scots and the Irish have a pretty clear idea of it.'

'I would guess that ninety per cent of the inhabitants of this country couldn't tell you the correct name of the country. The United Kingdom of something-or-other.'

'The name is a twentieth-century bureaucratic invention. These things take time.'

'And nobody seems to know whether you're Europeans or not.'

'That has become a hot political question.'

'Your semi-attachment and semi-detachment from the EU?'

'Before that, everyone knew we were European. Even Henry VIII, a Renaissance king and devout Catholic, Defender of the Faith. He detached us from the Roman Church, the EU of its day, for personal reasons. But we were still a full member of Europe as a culture and dominated it diplomatically.'

'And nobody knows whether to be proud of the British Empire or ashamed of it.'

'That's another recent thing. People made fun of Queen Victoria calling herself Empress of India. There were jingoists who thought of us as a second Roman Empire on which the sun never set. And there were hard-headed people, especially in the City of London, who knew that the empire was really an economic thing, using much of the rest of the world as suppliers of things we needed, and consumers of the things we had to sell.'

'They wave flags and sing Rule Britannia

with gusto at the last night of the Proms, don't they?'

'I think everyone has a sort of imperial nostalgia, nostalgia for the days when we truly were a great power in the world.'

'I can understand that. It was the two world wars that ended it all. And *pax Americana* replaced *pax Britannica*.'

'You Americans helped us to avoid *pax Germanica*. But you'd been gunning for the British empire since you started to see yourselves as a great power after your Civil War. You saw that undermining the British global economy was the way to do it, rather than war. But it turned out that war did the trick for you.'

'It's strange that your politicians still talk about a special relationship between the UK and the US. It's special in the sense of being unique, not in any sentimental sense, surely.'

'It's a diplomatic fantasy which politicians use rhetorically when it might be useful. But you're right, it is a unique relationship.'

'That's something that puzzles me, Nick – if I may. Britain created the United States from nothing and, whatever you may think of what the Americans have made of it, that's a pretty big claim to fame, I would have thought.'

'English people are almost entirely ignorant of history. The Scots, the Welsh and the Irish are keenly conscious of their history, because it's mostly the story of English oppression and abuse and general superciliousness.'

'You might have thought that inventing a very sane form of English religion and inventing liberal democracy, the scientific revolution and the industrial revolution would make any other nation feel proud.'

'We're unusual in not having caught the bug of nationalism in the nineteenth century, which wreaked such havoc in continental Europe. We're a mongrel people ourselves. And we've always welcomed immigrants coming from other countries with their own ideas and useful skills.'

'I'll tell you why you were spared from the bug of nationalism, Nick. In one word. Shakespeare.'

'Convince me, Jack.'

'Shakespeare invented a form of English nationalism that was something more than nationalism. It was the self-consciousness of a society that had no need to explain its origin, no need to justify its institutions, no need to compare itself with foreigners. A sort of supernationalism. *This other Eden. Demi-paradise. This happy breed of men. This blessed plot. The envy of less happy lands. This England.*'

'Over-the-top words spoken by someone trying to justify getting rid of Richard II.'

'That's exactly my point. Shakespeare simply assumed a higher order that kings were failing to respect. But what higher order? Where did it come from? A constitution seemed to exist as a sort of natural phenomenon like the weather. From 1066 you contrived always to have non-English kings. French, Welsh, Scottish, Dutch, German.'

'They've certainly been a mixed bag. We've only called one of them Great. And that was King Alfred who died in the year 899.'

'Only the English could say when kings were violating this mystical invisible constitution. And so you got rid of Richard II, Charles I, and James II. And you got King John to put his seal on a Magna Carta in 1215, supposedly containing various ancient rights of the English people.'

'George Washington's father had to emigrate from England after his father had taken the royal side in the English Civil War. Thomas Jefferson invoked the Anglo-Saxon rights and liberties of the English people to justify getting rid of the British government from America. Later he insisted on adding a Bill of Rights to the US Constitution. Not a good idea.'

'Why not? Things would have been much worse without it.'

'All such human rights documents are open to the objection that they turn the ultimate high values of a society into the plaything of lawyers, so that high values lose their power to override all law and government, leaving the society with no ultimate high values. The most precious human values become legal rights and duties of the citizen.'

'There speaks the voice of the British Home Office, I guess.'

'Its better voice, not its only voice.'

'But what on earth was the British constitutional order, Nick? It wasn't a monarchy. The kings were not absolute, like kings on the continent. It wasn't a republic because it had a king. It wasn't a democracy because parliament was a conspiracy between the City of London in the House of Commons and the great landowners in the House of Lords. The two main stakeholders in the national economy.'

'Someone the whole show seemed to muddle on through thick and thin.'

'That's the greatest mystery of all. Operating this ramshackle unconstitutional constitutional order was the work of amateurs. Your prime ministers were always amateurs, usually great landowners who saw England as the macro version of their own estates which they governed as micro-monarchs.'

'Often benevolently, it has to be said.'

'Because they depended on the labour and the allegiance of their tenants. Even your class-system is ingenious. Everyone has someone they can look down on, but inferior people feel contempt for superior people.'

'A nineteenth century commentator on what he called the English constitution, one of the founders of the *Economist* newspaper, said that our system depended on the stupidity of the British people, who had no idea who really runs the country behind the fantasy monarchy. Voltaire said it was a republic hiding in the skirts of a monarchy.'

'At least you didn't suffer the fate of the Greek city-states who took to fighting each other and went into decline.'

'We used force for centuries to keep the Scots

and the Irish under English control. Until 1746, in the case of Scotland. Until the twentieth century, in the case of Ireland.'

'I was wrong, Nick. The greatest mystery of all is not your mystical constitution but how on earth you acquired your empire, a worldwide empire bigger than the Roman Empire. It seems to have been done absent-mindedly, not merely by force. People invested in groups of adventurers wandering round the world looking for opportunities for profit. London-based companies settled unasked in foreign countries. And somehow those companies were taken over by the British government, and those countries became colonies.'

'The Spanish the Portuguese and the Dutch and the French were doing the same thing, Jack.'

'The British have been an amazingly war-making people. But Parliament's control of the financing of war means that you always fought wars for good practical reasons. The people had to pay for the war, so the expense had to be justified. Not like Louis XIV or Frederick the Great, simply asserting the power of France and Prussia.

'The American Revolutionary War divided opinion in England. The American colonies didn't produce much that we needed, even if they were useful consumers of our exports. Many people thought it was not worth the effort to try to keep them under our control.'

'You lost the American colonies absent-mindedly, Nick. A lapse of judgment by amateur prime ministers.'

'An odd thing is that we have always felt culturally inferior to our continental neighbours. The French have always thought of us as barbarians, uncivilised, a sort of local Wild West, eating roast-beef and getting drunk.'

'You've had great scientists and great engineers, practical people, and that must be more important. Your civilisation is a different kind of civilisation.'

'But think of the amazing high culture of Italy, Jack, in every field, or the elegant refinement of French civilisation, so that French civilisation became an ideal for the whole of Europe. And think of the cultural richness of the hundreds of German mini-states before they were unified in the nineteenth century, with their professional musicians and opera-houses and universities. And yet it was Goethe who understood the particular nature of the British better than anyone.'

'You lived in a modern world centuries before the modern world existed. British people don't realise how much they owe to British philosophers, who were practical people in their own way. They transformed continental philosophy, as Kant and Goethe said. They made the best ideas about how human beings should live in society, a metaphysical constitution above and beyond the physics of the mystical constitution of government.'

'I sometimes think that the Rule of Law may be one of our greatest achievements. The idea that all public power is under the law applied and enforced by independent courts.'

'Correct me if I'm wrong, Nick. But wasn't that also a product of chance?'

'Yes. You mean the presence of the Inns of Court in London, medieval guilds of practising lawyers, meant that there was an independent legal profession, independent of the monarch and government. And lawyers came to be well-represented in the House Commons. Kings James I and Charles I thought the king was the source of the law and above the law. The lawyers told him that they were kings because of the law, and they were under the law, like everyone else.'

'And that idea became a fundamental principle of liberal democracy across the world. Tell me, Nick. How did Britain avoid getting a written constitution? After 1789, everyone everywhere got written constitutions.'

'We did have such a thing under Oliver Cromwell. The Instrument of Government of 1653, creating a republic. It lasted until 1660. It even contained a separation of powers, which did for Cromwell in the end. He couldn't control Parliament. Several of our American colonies had written constitutions. Virginia even had a Bill of Rights.'

'You might say that the American Constitution put the unwritten British constitution into writing. Or one idea of it, as Americans understood it in 1787. And then the French put in writing a republican constitution in 1793, ditching more than a thousand years of absolute monarchy.'

'We've learned a lot about the problems of written constitutions since then, haven't we, Jack?'

'In America we're stuck with an eighteenth-century constitution trying to run a twenty-first century society. The dominant social classes designed the 1787 constitution to limit direct democracy as much as possible and to prevent the return of monarchy, and to leave them as the dominant classes. The checks and balances are so ingenious that it makes government very difficult and a coherent foreign policy impossible.'

'And a president with a majority in both Houses of Congress is as close to a monarch as dammit, as we've seen recently, Jack.'

'It seems to me that there's an important thing we've learned about written constitutions, Nick. They're very friendly to autocrats and dictators. If they pack the highest court with their friends and use the suspending powers and the emergency powers, everything they do is legally justified. And they can amend the constitution to make it even more convenient. Then the Rule of Law means the rule of the ruler through law.'

'Yes. The Third Reich was very legalistic. Soviet Russia had a nice written constitution.'

'So now, Nick, tell me how on earth the British constitutional dystopia managed to survive, and to make what I believe is a utopia compared with all other countries that I know.'

'I'm afraid that question may be a bit above my pay grade. But I think the main thing is that British society could change non-stop, and mostly progress, for fifteen centuries. We were never static, unlike so many other countries. Beginning in the thirteenth century Parliament could make social change into instant law. If my memory serves, the Tudor monarchs used thirty-seven Acts of Parliament to make the Reformation. And we trusted the courts to keep the common law in step with changes in society, with as little political bias as possible.'

'And Parliament somehow became more and more democratic, didn't it?'

'The Duke of Wellington told the House of Lords to support giving the vote to the property-owning middle-class in 1832. Property-owners favour stability. He said Britain was doing revolution by process of law. So we avoided the revolutions that devastated so many continental countries in the nineteenth century. Engels said the British Parliament was the most revolutionary body in Europe in the nineteenth century.'

'And, in the century of relative peace after 1815, your warrior spirit was diverted into an obsession with competitive games with complicated rules, most of which you invented. Soccer and rugby and cricket and horse-racing and snooker and golf and croquet and lawn tennis and lawn bowls and bridge and pub quizzes. Played with total commitment.'

'And national politics became the biggest game of all, Jack. It's only fairly recently that professional cricketers have stopped being divided into so-called gentlemen and players. In the nineteenth century, politics was played by both gentlemen and players. Now it is only played by players.'

'Some people objected to giving the vote to the lower orders, didn't they? They said it was giving power to the uneducated.'

'In the 1860's the whole education system was reformed by Parliament, under the slogan "we must educate our masters".'

'But the upper classes went on being educated in public schools that were not public, didn't they, Nick?'

'No one can rule who has not himself been ruled. That was the Victorian principle. The public schools taught future rulers how to suffer and how to be arrogant. And a bit of Greek and Latin. And they went out to rule impossible places, sustained by gin and tonic. An undergraduate friend of mine went out to rule northern Nigeria at the age of thirty.'

'Europeans have the wrong idea about America. They suppose that it's Europe transported across the water. But it isn't. It's an utterly different civilisation. A matriarchy in the home, so that men have to act out their virility and dominance outside the home, especially in business and politics and crime, with a lot of swearing and drinking, and an obsession with the ultimate Freudian symbol of displaced virility, the gun.'

'The Puritan theocracy lives on, doesn't it, Jack, despite everything.'

'Only distantly, Nick. Religion in America has a much more masculine ethos than religion in Europe. Even Catholic priests have a more macho and assertive style. My grandparents were traditional Italian Catholics.'

'Billy Graham used to say that competition among religions was a good thing, like competition in capitalism. It makes them try harder. In Europe the competition is between religion and indifference.'

'In many American Gods we trust. Some of them are very big business, Nick. Making millions. Some of them were invented out of nothing by men, like producing a new breakfast cereal or a new automobile.'

'I once saw a TV advert in California for one of the big televangelists. "Remember, friends, your gift of love is tax-deductible." I suppose it's a better selling-point than the vague promise of an after-life.'

'A new twist on medieval Indulgences. Europeans try to form a coherent image of America, Nick. No hope. A marriage of submission to religion and the Wild West's rejection of authority, whether it comes from Washington or the local sheriff, whom they elect to office, to keep tabs on them.'

'And yet Europeans see ordinary Americans as open, generous, and polite. Compared with Europeans. Every British visitor says that. No conifer hedges around their gardens or around their minds.'

'Americans act out the role of being good Americans all their lives. They learn Americanism in school. Saluting the flag. Pledge of Allegiance. Hand on the heart. Immigrants master it by the second generation. Socialism is Communism under another name. An unamerican activity. Right-wing Catholics in America oppose what they see as the new socialising of Catholicism.'

'Hollywood in its glory days gave the world a

white picket-fence Doris Day image of America. Now films and TV give the world a very dark picture.'

'Both of them fantasies, Nick. If you were to ask me, I would say that Americans see ordinary English people as warm-hearted and natural and rather lazy. If you ever finally get to know them, if you get through their Maginot lines of self-defence. What the English really like is a quiet life. The British psyche seems to have remained the same through all the centuries of endless change. Explain the British psyche to me, Nick.'

'An English person is the last person to answer that question. The nearest you would get is something in the philosophy of the Scottish Enlightenment. The Scots are more thoughtful people. The philosophy of common sense. The idea that human beings share sensible general ideas that help us to reach collective decisions and moral judgments. And we think we see that in American politics at its best.'

'The British were the first country to make public opinion into a fourth organ of the constitution, weren't they?'

'For fifteen hundred years, after the Romans left, we've had immigrants from everywhere coming to live here. But we developed what

French philosophers call a vigorous collective consciousness through endless talk. It's what German philosophers call the real constitution. Who actually rules the rulers?'

'A lot of it outside Parliament, wasn't it? Involving ordinary people. Tom Paine was the prophet of the American and French Revolutions. Robert Owen invented socialism before Marx and Engels had written a word about it. Aspects of common sense, I suppose.'

'There were dozens of newspapers already at the beginning of the eighteenth century, Jack. There were five hundred coffee-houses in London at that time, where people talked and talked. Lloyds insurance and the stock market started in coffee-houses.'

'The British empire was started by pressure from below, private enterprise, rather than power imposed from above.'

'That has been the main source of social progress in Britain. To make a modern society you have to have a self-confident and aspiring middle-class. And we've had that since the fourteenth century.'

'And pressure from below is as much a form of representative government as elections and Parliament, isn't it, Nick?'

'Yes. The intimate sharing of important values, and lively competition among values. Politics at the level of society. Not merely at the level of government.'

'Is that still true? Your blessed country seems to be full of confrontation now, and corruption of all kinds, and crude populism and selfish individualism.'

'Everything depends on the next generations of young people, Jack. If they turn out to be sober and sensible and generous, then the country can be saved yet again. That, and the survival of native common sense, despite everything.'

'Any day now I will be a British-American dual national, a citizen of your beautiful country and your impossible dystopian utopia.'

'And you will be very welcome, Jack. But just remember, in England we don't talk to strangers on trains.'

MORAL
It takes a foreigner to understand another country.

* * *

Twenty-One

THE HUMAN BEINGS' TALE

A SPECIES FACING EXTINCTION
Homo neque sapiens

You can tell a lot about a country by its food. Everyone knows that. You can tell a lot about a country by its national television. If it's a country you are particularly fond of, you may choose to dismiss its national television, which will certainly be abysmal, as an unfortunate aberration due to capitalism.

You can tell a lot about a country by its churches, both as buildings and as institutions. All of these things give us crucial information in the dimensions of both space and time. Countries change. Some things survive. Memory incarnates the past in people and in the things that survive.

In Europe, we are fortunate to have thirty-something countries, all wonderfully different and proud of it, but also hundreds of sub-countries and tribes and peoples, all different and proud of the fact. Mr Heineken, whose family lent its name to an excellent beer, counted them all, and found that there are, indeed, hundreds of tribes in Europe. He thought that all of them should be recognised in a true European union.

An Indian friend told me that the same is true of other countries, especially countries that may seem to be monolithic. Like India and China and Russia and Brazil. Not to mention the U.S. of A.

'The United States,' he said, 'is a fiction of fractions and factions and frictions.'

Ignoring the rather forced euphony of his remark, that was surely nothing but the truth.

'Extrapolating to the global level,' my Indian friend continued, 'there must be tens of thousands of countries and tribes and peoples, all of them with their own history, all of them different, and proud of the difference.'

'It does make you wonder,' I said, 'if the human race is nothing but a fiction of fractions and factions and frictions.'

'It would explain a lot about human history whose general awfulness is, otherwise, an enigma contained in a mystery.'

'I think you mean human historiography,' I said. 'The historians have to have something to write about. And war and human conflict make a good story.'

'You're right. Talking about peace, plenty and general happiness would not sell books, or get you tenure at a university.'

'The same is true of newspapers and television. A visitor from Mars would take one look at them and leave smartly. Not a species one would want to consort with.'

'Not to mention the social media,' my Indian friend said. 'Your hypothetical visitor from Mars would decide, within minutes, that we are a species that has gone mad, but seems not to know it.'

'I sometimes think about God,' I said.

'Don't we all?'

'You've got to feel some sympathy for him, if he exists. Created Man in his own image and likeness and look what we've turned out to be.'

'Let's hope he has other creations elsewhere,' my Indian friend said. 'Doing better. Otherwise, he'd be a very sad God indeed, and that can't be a good thing. He might wreak thunderbolts and plagues and famines.'

'Perhaps that explains climate change. God has lost patience and wants us to fry in our own juice.'

Sorry, I got distracted. I should have introduced myself. Hi. I'm Matthew Broad. I'm a retired academic. Not that academics ever retire. They just stop being paid. I'm from Durham, England. I don't think we've met.

In America, when you're introduced, the other party repeats your name, so that they're more likely to remember it. In England, we can know people for years, talk to them in the pub every week, without knowing their name. However, on the other hand, we are terribly sensitive in interpreting signals. We know a great deal about other people without being told.

We know someone's social class within seconds. They need only speak three or four words. We know someone's degree of education within minutes. Do they speak in sentences, with subject, verb, and object? The French speak in paragraphs. The Germans know the last word of a sentence when they begin it. For us English, a sentence is an adventure. Heaven knows where it may end up, if anywhere.

Clothes are a less reliable signal. Especially in the country, people tend to aspire to the appearance of a tramp, even if they live in a big house and have a big job. It's a matter of being considerate to other people's feelings. Nor does their car in the car park tell you very much. It may be a Land Rover that has seen better days, but of which one is fond, as if it were of a friend.

In the days when people talked to their neighbour in aeroplanes, the thing to do was to say to one's American neighbour: 'where are you from?' That could take care of most of the rest of the flight to New York. Where Americans are from is usually a complex matter. They move around so much, from coast to coast, and many places in-between. And they may be an immigrant, or have immigrant parents, and that's a whole other story.

You can tell a lot about a country from the formalities of their interpersonal relations. Think of the poor French and Germans, with their *Du* and *tu*. General de Gaulle addressed his wife as *vous,* until his dying day. And Goethe had views on the subject. Too much *Du* reflected a general decline in good manners in Germany. In England or America, you have to be Northern or Amish to use the word 'thou', unless you're quoting Shakespeare or the Bible.

Humanity will never reach the end of inventing ways to separate human beings and human societies from each other.

'Good manners,' I said. 'Does the idea still have any operative effect in society.'

'Manners is a patriarchal thing, Matthew,' my Indian friend said.

By the way, my Indian friend also has a name. Manu Narayan. Which is quite an up-market name, if you know your Sanskrit literature. He is what you might call a Wise Man.

'Manners are a matter of inherited norms,' Manu continued. 'And inherited norms must have been made by men. QED. Studying such things has been your job as an historian, Matthew.'

'Some of the most important norms are taken in with the mother's milk, during one's early Freud-doomed years. I don't know what happens if the mother's milk is formula. Could explain a lot about the modern world.'

'Everything depends on how you learn the dialectics of the Self and the Other, and the One and the Many. All human life is there. Me and You. Us and Them.'

'Isn't it amazing, and sad,' I said, 'how many words there are for what separates human beings from each other? Opposition, antipathy, division, discord, aggression, enmity, conflict, competition, dispute, battle, clash, struggle, nationalism, racism, genocide, sectarianism, persecution, and so on and on.'

'All of them the offspring of the fertile mating of Polemos and Hybris, not to mention the *coup de foudre* between Adam and Eve, or the carelessness of Pandora, or Ying and Yang. I've always admired your caste-system in Britain, Matthew.'

'We call it a class-system, and we're not supposed to admire it.'

'All Western countries have caste-systems. It's not based on a belief in the nature of the universe, like our caste-system in India. For you it's just a matter of fact, and that's that.'

'The Victorians prayed: "God bless the lowly in their station in life." And the lowly sang that lustily in hymns.'

'Most of your lowest class are comfortable with their station in life, Matthew. They have a healthy disdain for those to whom they touch their forelock. And with a bit of effort, and a lot of luck, they can ascend. From log-cabin to the White House. The middle class is permanently dissatisfied with its lot. All social progress is caused by the dissatisfaction of the middle class. Italy and Britain had the first active middle classes. And Italy and Britain led the way into the modern world.'

'But the supposed *scourge of inequality* has now become a huge hypocritical political mantra, Manu. Nobody is content with their lot any longer. Inequality means envy and struggle and strife. But nobody really believes that social and economic inequality will ever be overcome.'

'One more child of Polemos and Hybris.'

'I suppose you could say that all living things live thanks to the ongoing dialectic of life and death.'

'And, in the end, death wins, Matthew. All social life is dialectical, as Socrates told Plato, and we learned it from Plato. All social life is struggle.'

'I've never had much time for Hegel's idea that our idea of our self apparently means that we are bound to see each other as both master and slave. It was one of the roots of fascism. But it may be true psychologically that people can't fulfil themselves as a self except by mastering somebody else.'

'And the same would hold for whole societies and states and nations,' Manu said. 'Like Hegel's idea of the state as the ultimate human society, with the people making the state which possesses the people. And each state is complete in itself and competes with other states in equality and freedom, including the freedom of all of them from higher law or morality.'

'They're ghastly ideas. A licence for war and totalitarianism. But then the reality of the actual human world is rather ghastly.'

'Nowadays we're all supposed to be soft-hearted about Mother Nature, Matthew, whom we've so grievously wronged. That's a master-slave relationship, if ever there was one.'

'And it's a dialectical relation, Manu. We use Nature, and Nature does what it wants with us. Plagues and climate change and pollution and the exhaustion of natural resources. Nature says: enough and no more, wretched human race.'

'And there's a Self and Other problem with other living creatures. The avalanche of films about the creatures that share the planet with us has had an ambiguous effect on human consciousness. They're as much the product of evolution as we are, or as much the creation of God, but they're far too different from us to call them "my sisters the birds" without monumental hypocrisy. A lot of them are monstrously peculiar. No serious God or intelligent design could have created them.'

'Animals do intelligent things, Manu. They speak to each other. They have feelings. They have families. They mourn. The social life of the ant makes human social life seem like child's play. They attack and kill each other in self-defence, rather than for no good reason, as we do.'

'But the human species is faced now with what people call global threats to which we've got to find global solutions. We're told that every day of the week. We're all in it together now. That's the progressive mantra, Matthew. Climate change, global economic collapse, global war. The human race has got to recognise its common identity, or we're doomed. So we're told.'

'Some hope, Manu! Religion used to be a way for people to rise above their diversities. But, in large parts of the world, the churches are in a losing battle with materialism. In Europe Christianity is marginal to people's lives.'

'And the big surviving religions are fiercely selfish, liable to contribute to division and enmity and persecution and discrimination, civil conflict, and even war, and they're all full of sectarianism and dissention within themselves.'

'I would add another myth, Manu, to your myth about our supposed identity with Nature. It's a contradictory myth. The myth of individualism. People say that individualism is a great achievement after centuries of human oppression and exploitation and colonialism. But people also say that the selfishness at the heart of capitalism is ruining the world. And that causes a third myth, the myth of populism, the ridiculous claim that ordinary people are now ruling the world or should rule the world.'

'The social media show all three sides of that myth, Matthew. And they themselves have become yet another big source of division and hatred.'

'Togetherness is now an ultimate apartness.'

'We seem to have talked ourselves into a bit of a corner, Matthew.'

'Not to say a brick wall, a dead end, a very vicious circle. And do you know what, Manu? That's the feeling of everybody now. Not despair, but total and utter confusion about the human condition and its future. And not just in Britain. Everywhere.'

'The human race united at last. In ultimate existential confusion.'

'What an irony, Manu! What a paradox! The human race united at last in hopelessness.'

'Is it possible that such an improbable thing could actually bring about a transformation in the human condition?'

'It would involve a new and hugely improbable form of human humility, Manu. The new humanism of the Renaissance, and then the arrogance of the French Enlightenment. In the nineteenth century, they became a form of ultimate human triumphalism, under the impact of the discoveries and wonders of the natural sciences.'

'Human omnipotence without God's infinite wisdom,' Manu said. 'There's nothing that human beings cannot do. No problem they cannot solve. And that idea was exported across the world in the baggage of imperialism. Despite the total and profound inequality of the imperial world, we all belonged to that amazing species called the human species. Nothing was impossible for any of us, even if might take time to achieve it.'

'Progress had become inevitable. And

unavoidable, even if might steam-roller into oblivion ancient cultures and ways of living.'

'Capitalism became the great steam-engine of unstoppable human progress.'

'And there was no longer any religion or philosophy to make it humane, Manu. For the first time in human history, there was nothing to civilise civilisation.'

'Maybe, rather late in the day, Herbert Marcuse could be the guru for a world united in existential hopelessness. The one-dimensional human mind, made one by the pressures of industrialism and capitalism and the total social control of modern society, could only think collectively, no longer individually.'

'The French call it *pensée unique* or single thought, Manu. Social pressure to have only one view on controversial questions. Like political correctness or woke cancelling.'

'The human species can do anything, except live together in peace and friendship and common decency.'

'The paradox and irony is that, if existential despair is now the one-dimensional thought and the single thought of all human beings, then it may be the basis of a new idea of a shared identity of the human species.'

'The ancient Greeks and the Romans believed in the idea of humanity, Manu. Socrates said he was not a citizen of Athens. He said he was a citizen of the world.'

'And the Greeks and Romans believed in humanity as a virtue. Humaneness. Fellow-feeling. Altruism. Give or take slavery, of course.'

'Who knows, Manu? Perhaps there could be yet another Renaissance. A new Enlightenment. A new humanism. A new religion. The human species getting to know itself at last for what it really and truly and honestly is. The bright light and the awful darkness. The end of the grand human illusion.'

'Even if you and I were able to believe that ourselves, Matthew, other people would say that we were out of our minds.'

'Great ideas start as madness. Great ideas have always been thought before. They are proved when they are used to fill a mental void, when their time has come.'

'That time has come,' Manu said. 'Like never before in human history. Human beings now know that their so-called omnipotence is capable of causing the end of civilisation and the extinction of the species.'

'The species that failed to adapt to challenges that it made for itself. An ironical end to Evolution by Natural Selection.'

'The unsurvival of the unfit.'

MORAL
Meet the Ultimate Achievement
of Evolution. And run for your life!

* * *

Twenty-Two

THE TECH WIZARD'S TALE

RESCUING HUMANITY FROM ITSELF
A revolution in the mind

'Why has the human species made such a mess of its brief presence on the planet Earth?'

Who has not asked that question at some time in their lives?

Few try to find an answer. Even fewer try to do something about it.

If you are trained as a scientist or an engineer, you know that there must be an answer to every question about the natural world, and nothing is impossible in meeting the challenges of the physical world. A problem is simply something that hasn't yet been solved.

Gavin Meredith is a scientist and an engineer. He has done well out of it. He has made a lot of money. He would tell you that he has not allowed money to corrupt him. He has stayed true to the values of the modest family which allowed him and encouraged him to do well whatever he chose to do.

The time had come, in his life, to ask himself the great question about the human species from the point of view of a scientist or an engineer.

Gavin Meredith does not count his money, or keep it in sacks under his bed, or brag about it in people magazines. He organises his appearances in the mass media, so far as anyone can. He has accountants who seem to be efficient at looking after, and cautiously increasing, his wealth.

He has a modest house in Palo Alto, in the shadow of the modestly Hispanic buildings of the very unmodest Stanford University. Not for him a mansion in Malibu overlooking State Route 1 and the scrawny Malibu beach, or a mansion in Hollywood looking down on the air pollution of Los Angeles. He doesn't have a penthouse in New York. When he is there, and he is usually glad to be there, he stays at the Harvard Club.

One thing he does insist on is the correct pronunciation of his surname. Stress on the second syllable. A clue there. He is Welsh and proud of it.

The Welsh were in the land of Gavin's fathers long before the English were in Angleland. Saint

David took Christianity from Wales all over the place, including England and France. Gavin is a Celtic Briton, a living representative of one of the world's oldest and most sophisticated cultures. He will say all of this, with some vigour, especially if people call him English.

He returns as often as possible to the land of his fathers, where he is a visiting professor in the Computer Science Department of the University of Aberystwyth.

In at the beginning of facial recognition technology, he was one of the first to make big money out of something that has become an everyday thing. His work in Cambridge in applied mathematics led him into computer technology in its early days. He developed some of the original facial recognition algorithms in the earliest forms of its technology. In those days, he was not required to give the university a share in his patents.

He had also been a pioneer in cyber security, and its related field of cybersurveillance in the detection of crime. After 9/11, he has worked closely and profitably with the US Department of Defense and the Department of Homeland Security in the so-called war on terror. A paranoid government spends money generously.

He sold his three main companies before the global financial crisis of 2008. His work in all these fields continues intermittently, in a cyber world which is now more frenzied than ever and, as he says, close to global implosion.

It was at Cambridge that he had first begun to think about the nature of his mind, that is to say, the nature of the mind of someone who practises natural science or engineering as their way of life. It separates them dramatically from those who seek truth by other means, or who work with their imagination, or who accept the truth from religious dogma, or people who do not use their minds in making a living.

Natural science and engineering involve an intensely constraining use of the mind, with protocols governing the conduct of natural science and engineering acting as absolutes, a law of the Medes and Persians. Violation of the rules will be found out sooner or later. There is also an intrinsic element of imagination, a specialised form of imagination involved in choosing new problems to deal with and seeing new avenues to follow to make progress, to recognise new truth when you see it.

Gavin Meredith and Helen Green got to know each other through the interdisciplinary nature of their college in Cambridge. They married soon after graduation. She had read history for her degree and had specialised thereafter in the political history of various countries, including the United States, teaching in various universities as she accompanied Gavin in his displacements.

'Why have you never written about the theory of history,' Gavin had asked her on one occasion, 'or even the philosophy of history, if there is such a thing?'

'Historians only do that when they're old,' Helen said. 'When they've given up doing serious work. They nail their past work to the mast of one of the many competing theories of history, to justify themselves retrospectively.'

'So historians themselves don't know what history is!'

'Heavens, no. Some of them think that it's a form of science, a sort of human entomology. The facts, only the facts. Some of them think it's an art-form, an imaginative reconstruction of the bits and pieces that survive from the past to make a convincing story. Some of them think it's inevitably ideological, putting a spin on the past to serve the interests of a dominant class. And so on. Herodotus *versus* Thucydides.'

'It seems strange to me that historians take such a relaxed attitude to their work. Surely, they're dealing with the troubled history of the human species. You'd think they would be on the front line of people seeking to improve the world. And history, whether fact or fantasy can have huge real-world effects.'

'Not all of them have been relaxed, Gavin. Edward Gibbon said that history is nothing but the register of the crimes, follies, and misfortunes of mankind. And Voltaire said the same thing, and he said that we only seem to like history when it takes the form of tragedy. And Hegel said that the periods of happiness are the blank pages of history. And they were three great historians.'

'And did they try to do anything about it?'

'Hegel and Voltaire certainly did.'

For Gavin, his cross-examination of Helen on this matter was intimately related to his own anguished self-questioning about the nature of the minds that practise natural science or engineering.

'From what you say, Helen, being a historian seems a million miles from what me and my kind do for a living,'

'C.P. Snow called it the two cultures, Gavin. In

the 1950's. He blamed traditional education for creating two intellectual worlds of the sciences and the humanities. He said that humanities people know as little about physics as Neolithic man.'

'Yes,' Gavin said. 'And that led to a massive movement to publish popular science magazines and put popular science programme on TV.'

'But has that meant that humanities people really know much or understand much about science? I wonder, Gavin. I'm not sure.'

'I don't wonder, Helen. I'm sure. The answer is: no. Science is extremely specialised and complex nowadays. I'm not sure how many nuclear physicists understand molecular biology and vice versa. And electronic engineering is a series of black boxes. and very few people know anything much about what's inside those black boxes. For most people now, science and electronic engineering are modern forms of magic. Magic that works wonders, but hardly anyone knows how.'

'In the humanities, there's the same kind of thing,' Helen said. 'Historians have become more and more specialised. Even good historians know more and more about less and less. And nobody knows much about other people's fields of study. And avalanches of books and articles are published that very few people are likely to read, or to read in the old-fashioned thorough way.'

'And the general public only gets a dumbed down version of history in books written by journalists or amateur historians or TV documentaries or historical fiction or films. Which must be galling for you professional historians.'

'Snow's two cultures have become no culture, Gavin. No one knowing much about anything.'

'The mass of popular science put before the public has had two effects. It has made ordinary people worship scientists and engineers as superhuman beings, taking the place of astrologers and alchemists and shamans, with arcane knowledge that ordinary people can't argue with.'

'Producing marvels and wonders,' Helen said, 'some of which make human life better, and some of which make it worse.'

'Yes. And the second effect is that scientists and engineers come to believe that their omnipotence makes other forms of knowledge redundant. Any problem can be solved by some solution in science or engineering. And there are signs now that some of them think that this Brunelesque state of mind could be applied to the problems of human society and human life in general.'

'Governments and existing social systems have failed. Leave the whole thing to us strictly rational people.'

'They think they are followers of the amazing Francis Bacon who saw that the essence of science is its method. Nature to be commanded must be obeyed. Hence the humility of scientists in their everyday work, in the face of intractable natural reality. Religion and philosophy are not part of that method.'

'I love a thing Bacon said, Gavin. From a natural philosophy, pure and unmixed, better things are to be expected. Or words to that effect. The most splendid understatement ever, given the subsequent wonders and marvels produced by natural science.'

'But people, especially scientists, forget something else that Bacon said. He said that if anyone thinks that philosophy and universality are idle studies, they are forgetting that all professions are served and supplied by them. Or words to that effect.'

'The French Enlightenment treated Bacon

as its presiding genius,' Helen said, 'because he had called for a total reconstruction of sciences, arts, and all human knowledge upon proper foundations. And he said that already in 1620! It took the French more than a century to do what Bacon suggested, in their massive Encyclopaedia, covering the whole of human knowledge at that time. The French Enlightenment.'

'We need a new Enlightenment now. Online, of course. A total reconstruction of Wikipedia.'

The skeleton conversation presented here reflects a small part of a concern on Gavin's part that has gone far beyond the problems of culture and the methods of science and engineering. Why is the world as it is? How could it be made better in the future? A familiar form of question for a scientist or an engineer.

This has become the subject of other conversations between Gavin and Helen. And Gavin has discussed it with other serious scientists and engineers, to the extent that they have sometimes come to regard him as obsessed. For some of them, these are unrealistic questions in themselves, capable of no useful answer. The problems of the world are an accumulation of micro problems. Not amounting to any meaningful macro problem.

'Contrary to popular belief,' Helen said on another occasion, 'ideas rule the world, and ideas have always ruled the world. People think that people of power rule the world, but people of power have always been ruled by ideas.'

'For most of human history, those ideas came from religion, didn't they, Helen? People of power could justify their power by a religion that they didn't invent, but which they could easily manipulate in their own interest.'

'And which their subjects accepted on blind trust.'

'As religion declined, its place was taken by ideologies which performed the same function in binding a society together, legitimating the power of the powerful.'

'Which their subjects accepted on blind trust. Absolutist monarchy and democracy and capitalism and nationalism and communism and fascism and scientific absolutism.'

'Which leads to an obsessive and agonising question, Helen, a question that is now a painfully topical question. What happens if both religion and ideology lose their power, as seems to be happening now? What keeps society together then? What rules the world then?'

'And you have tried to begin to answer those questions, Gavin. You wrote an article for *Prospect* magazine. *A World Ruled by Interacting Systems.* That was your title.'

'Yes. My idea was that everyone now, rulers and subjects, are dominated by autonomic systems that they don't control, which they can only seek to manipulate to their advantage. Global economic systems. The populist global public mind. The inventions that science and engineering happen to produce randomly, including benevolent inventions and deadly inventions.'

'Climate change is the *ne plus ultra* of an autonomous event, isn't it?'

'Yes. But perhaps even more worrying than climate change is the age-old problem of war caused by the autonomic interacting of states, war that no one in their right mind could want nowadays, because it would probably be world war, and nuclear war or bacteriological war or cyber war, or all four, which no one could prevent. The outbreak of war is always triggered by smaller random events.'

'World war as the ultimate and final autonomous interacting system of the self-harming and self-destroying of the human species. You said that in your *Prospect* article. But now, recently, you have gone further in your perfectly reasonable doom-mongering, haven't you? Professor Meredith becomes Dr Pangloom.'

'I'm almost in despair, but not quite.'

'I know one of your inconceivable solutions. And I am not at all sure that it's impossible. The total reconstruction of the nature of education.'

'The idea is that some centibillionaires or billionaires or mere millionaires, who are also intelligent and public-spirited, might get together to make possible a new form of education. It would be designed to produce the best possible kind of human being to live in the best possible kind of human society. The best minds have been thinking about education as long as high-level thinking has existed.'

'Which might suggest that it's unlikely to be transformed now, in our particularly benighted and uncultured times. The ultimately rich seem more interested in escaping from the planet Earth into a new world in space.'

'That's madness. They should devote their unstoppable energy and their ruthless ambition to helping poor suffering humanity in its hour of terminal need.'

'I'm keen on your idea that a central feature of the new education would be to study how ideas make human reality. And how better ideas might make a better human reality.'

'Yes. We would establish professorships of social philosophy at all the leading universities, making make their effect trickle down to the schools, preparing the young to be the best at whatever they choose to do in life. And to be the best kind of human being. And the new education would continue as life-time education. Education is not only for the young.'

'I'm sure your new form of education will take up the wise words of Francis Bacon. It could help those scientists and engineers who disdain the humanities to understand that their work depends on the human world that it's the business of the humanities to study and hopefully to improve.'

'It would let them share the great intellectual excitement of the humanities, Helen. Discovering the history of how the human world was made by theory and practice and imagination. Deconstructing and dissecting how it is now. and how it could be in the future.'

'The humanities might gain a lot from the cool and calm and patient and orderly and rational gaze of scientists and engineers. Another of your supposedly inconceivable panaceas is that the universal religions might remember their responsibility towards actual human beings living their brief lives here on Earth.'

'It should be the essence of what religions are there to do. Their job is to insert the transcendental into the very untranscendental human condition. To make us think higher and further than the everyday mess of things. To transform human beings into something better, so that human societies can become something better. And, my God, don't we need that now!'

'I'm not so sure about your third inconceivable remedy, Gavin.'

'It's simply the belief that the vast mass of human beings, ordinary human beings, are decent people, with an intuitive sense of right and wrong, regardless of the rampant immorality and amorality and stupidity of those who rule their lives politically and economically and mentally.'

'Do you suppose that such people could rise *en masse*, Gavin, and destroy their destroyers? That does seem a bit unlikely.'

'But not impossible, Helen.'

'Revolutions have usually been made by the

bourgeoisie, not the mass of the people. And, very often, the condition of the mass of the people has been worse after the revolution than before.'

'There are revolutions and revolutions, Helen. What I've got in mind is a revolution in the mind, not in the streets. Progress in the human condition has been the result of better ideas taking effect in practice.'

'From thesis to praxis, as Hegel or Karl Marx would say.'

'And, my God, don't we need better ideas now?'

'And I think you think that you already have a textbook for the new and improved brand of thesis and praxis.'

'Two textbooks, actually. I came across an author I'd never heard of. Philp Allott. His book *Eutopia* takes up the challenge set by Thomas More five centuries ago. To think about a better world, invoking the collected wisdom of thoughtful people throughout human history. And his *Eusophia* imagines how a group of intelligent and public-spirited rich and powerful people might intervene in the world to make it better, inspired by a sense of despair at the present state of things, and a feeling for an unfulfilled human ideal.'

'Imagination is the ultimate human freedom. No harm in hoping.'

'And then I had a vision.'

'You had a vision. Gavin's vision.'

'I saw a garden with two small Doric temples facing each other. A Temple of Human Power, with statues representing Science and Government and Money. A Temple of Human Wisdom, with statues representing Love and Hope and Peace. And, between them, a fountain with a Janus-figure of a child. One face smiling. One face weeping. The sound of the fountain is the music of time.'

'They must have been very old temples.'

'Very old. Timeless. But perfectly preserved.'

'You've come a long way from computer technology, Gavin.'

'I've grown up, Helen.'

MORAL
Scientists and engineers can imagine.

* * *

Twenty-Three

THE GARDENER'S TALE

CULTIVATE YOUR GARDEN
The simple life, if all else fails

I garden, therefore I am. I have always gardened. It follows that I am not Candide. I have not needed a Turkish wise man telling me to reject the meaningless and hopeless human world, and to escape into myself.

But I am not Dr Pangloss or even Leibniz. Everything is not for the best in the best of all possible worlds. Far, far from it, at least in the possible world that is the actual world. Anyone with an ounce of common sense knows, from an early age, that the human world is meaningless and hopeless, until sometimes, and sometimes triumphantly, we ourselves give it meaning and purpose and hope. Even Voltaire knew that.

A garden is a lovesome thing, God wot! 'Tis very sure God walks in mine. It's not only God who wots this, or the poet. Any serious gardener knows it, and knows also that gardening is hard work.

God Almighty first planted a garden. It is the purest of human pleasures. We didn't need England's greatest philosopher to tell us this. We know it.

You don't have to be Gertrude Jekyll to be a serious gardener. An allotment will do. A window-box, even. You have to have it in your bones, not to mention your soul.

And what is it that you have to have? It's what Nietzsche perversely failed to call *the will to garden*, which is a will to power, but which is not only a power over living things, but also a power over yourself. It's a will to power that makes you humble, something that neither Nietzsche nor the Third Reich could imagine. *Nature to be commanded must be obeyed*, as the same great philosopher said, and he was also a philosopher of the garden.

I was led into these uncharacteristically profound thoughts when I was spending some time with my old friend Mollie Maine in Shropshire. A great gardener. A *jardinière nonpareille*.

Unfortunate that the word *jardinière* in French also means ornamental pot. The feminising obsession with orthography should have permitted the retention of the bi-gender original form. But who am I, an English amateur gardener, to offer advice to the mighty *Académie française*?

Mollie knows all that can reasonably be known about gardening, and she has a Royal Horticultural Society Gold Medal to prove it.

She and I started talking about the philosophy of gardening and then, as you will see, dear reader, we progressed somewhat beyond that in the philosophical direction.

'There's a preliminary question,' Mollie said. 'You have to decide which side you're on in the great English *versus* French existential dispute about the ideal garden. Natural or artificial? Natural, in the characteristically ambiguous English sense, of nature heavily guided by the hand of Man (or Woman). Artificial, only in the sense of being an imposition of the all-embracing rationality of Man (and Woman) which, the French believe, can rationalise anything from *jardinage* to *amour*.'

'Rousseau championed English gardening, didn't he, Mollie?'

'He had spent time in England. And people in the eighteenth century became quite fond of what they supposed were English gardens. *Jardin à l'anglaise. Englischer Garten. Giardino all'inglese.*'

'Marie Antoinette's English garden at Versailles was meant as balm for her troubled soul, wasn't it? And, heaven knows, she needed it, poor woman.'

'Didn't save her from the guillotine, James. Catherine the Great had an English garden too. Not much evidence that it made her feel humble, or even nice. Italian Renaissance gardens were a delightful half-way house. Not rigidly formal, but with special effects in architectural features and sculptures, often Greek or Roman. There's a lovely half-English one in Padua made by a man called Treves de' Bonfili. There are pictures of it in my book. You can visit it.'

'Francis Bacon was firmly on the natural side of the debate, wasn't he, Mollie? But he disapproved of garden ponds or statues in a garden. Mind you, he thought that a garden shouldn't be less than thirty acres, including woodland and a lake.'

'Not many people know that the Qing emperor in China in the eighteenth century favoured natural gardens. In my book, I quote a French Jesuit priest residing at the imperial court, writing in 1767 about the imperial garden. Hang on a moment. I'll get it.'

Mollie went to get her best-selling book of essays on gardening.

'Here we are. "The Chinese use art to improve nature with such success that an artist wins praise to the degree that his art does not show at all, and he has, rather, imitated nature." Great gardening minds think alike, you see.'

'I once visited Goethe's garden in Weimar,' I said. 'He was a keen gardener. Grew his own vegetables. Did a Darwin in his various botanical experiments, didn't he?'

'Goethe was obsessed by the idea that there must be an *Urpflanze* from which all other plants evolved. He went to the Alps to find it. No luck.'

'Darwin was a bit of the obsessional type, as well,' I said.

'You've seen his garden at Down House. It was an outdoor laboratory for him. He had an obsession with earthworms. He said that evolution wouldn't have been possible without earthworms. And he should know. Humble in the face of Nature, like you and me.'

'Darwin like me only in that respect, Mollie. There are bits of Nature that are my personal enemies, and I exercise my will to garden over them. Aphids, for example. They usually win. I approve of earthworms. They aerate the soil.'

'Darwin discovered that they bore underground horizontally for miles.'

'All the best empires have done gardening, haven't they, Mollie? Persia. Rome. Islam, Britain. I suppose it's because they were all highly civilised in some sense, despite all the rest.'

'If you have a garden and a library, you will want for nothing. As Cicero is alleged to have said. By means of our hands we struggle to create a second world within the world of nature. Our own private paradise. I can't remember who said that. I quote it in my lectures.'

That was it. My Damascus moment. My Candide/Pangloss moment.

'Is it possible,' I asked myself, in the last waking hour before falling asleep that night, when the mind is peculiarly creative, 'that gardening is a way we each give meaning and hope to a little world of our own. Could there be a larger message contained in that? The universal power of humility? A world ruled by modest ambition, and nothing more? A quietist world, content to make things tick along, and not much more?'

At breakfast the following morning, I told Mollie about my great night-thought, worthy of the breadth and depth of Edward Young.

'Great minds think alike, Philip,' Mollie said. 'I hadn't meant to tell you just yet. I've decided to give up all the RHS stuff, all my garden-design work, all the public speaking. Everything. Before it's too late, and I'm finally planted in the loam myself. I'm going to espouse the simple life. Sans everything. Except you, of course. And, hopefully, God.'

That led to a discussion about the meaning of the simple life.

I told Mollie that I had been doing a good deal of thinking about that matter recently. I told her that, in places as different as New York and Andalusia, I had discovered the absolute spiritual purity of the Here and Now. The present moment experienced in the present place to the exclusion of all else. Alone with God and Nature, in generic meanings of those two words. A rare and priceless thing.

'I think that has happened to me once or twice,' Mollie said, 'in very remote places, halfway up a snow-dusted mountain in Switzerland or a fjord in Norway. I didn't realise I was experiencing absolute spiritual purity, however.'

I told Mollie that I have a personal collection of examples of a simple life led by other people at different times in different places.

I used to go to a bar in New York, just off Broadway. You may think that New York is the ultimate negation of the simple life. But you should know that the teeming masses of New York are masses of fiercely separate individuals. Trying to survive and make good, or just trying to survive.

The bar was dark, with a TV high on a wall in one corner, with the sound turned down. People occasionally looked at it vaguely. I couldn't say whether it was the same people there every evening. Some of them looked like criminals, or members of what the Americans charmingly called organized crime, as if it at least has the merit of being organized.

They sat at the bar, talking intermittently and almost inaudibly to each other or a barman. The barman would take away an empty glass and say: 'another' or 'the same?' It was always the same. It was an hour or two of life at its simplest, without which the rest of life would not be bearable.

Once in Sardinia, I was staying at a campsite outside Olbia. It had a barbed wire fence around it. At night, a man with a rifle patrolled outside the fence. Protecting us from what. Animals? Bandits?

On a walk, I came across a herd of goats. I heard them before I saw them, with bells around their necks. They were followed by a man with a stick. They weaved their own way through the low pine trees growing out of the sand.

I saw the man several times after that. We exchanged greetings, respectful greetings, I believe. His was certainly a simple life, a life lived by his ancestors for thousands of years.

I visited Sutherland in the north-west of Scotland, surely one of the most beautiful places on Earth. You could walk for a day and not see another human being. Bliss. I was walking in the marshy ground, the foothills of Suilven.

I sat on a rock to have my lunch. Bottled water, sandwich, and a Mars Bar. A pure white horse was drinking at a nearby pool of water. It looked up. It turned its head to look at me, each of us looking at the other, animal to animal. Then we resumed our respective lunches.

That evening, in the bar of the hotel by the quayside in Lochinver, I met a trawlerman. Not the captain of a trawler. Just an ordinary trawlerman. For weeks on end, he left his family to do long-distance fishing in the North Atlantic, as far as Newfoundland. He'd done it since he was a youth, and he would do it until he could no longer drag the sea-soaked ropes. A simple life which, like the goatherd on Sardinia, his ancestors had lived for centuries.

I was staying at a tiny hotel in south-east Spain, owned by three brothers of purest Andalusian stock. Dignified and quiet in their manner. Not many clients, a few surfboarders, no restaurant. One evening I was having dinner in the next-door hotel. One of the brothers came in, carrying what was obviously a new-born baby, tiny, held gently in his strong loving arms.

He came over to show me the baby. I said the right kind of thing, I hope. Then he said that one of his brothers had just died of cancer of the thigh. I may have got the Spanish word wrong, but I think it was the thigh.

Birth and death and love together in one place at one time. There was not a tear in his eyes, eyes inherited from generations of hardship and suffering, lived in the love and fear of the Lord. There were tears in my eyes.

Once I stayed at a Cistercian monastery, run on the strictest of strict lines. No talking.

Meals pushed through a slot in the door of your cell. An occasional word stolen, and no doubt confessed to in Confession, as you tilled the ground or planted vegetables or harvested fruit or did some carpentry.

I tried to work out what effect this had had on the monks who, for all I knew, may have been accountants or car salesmen or ballet dancers in a former life. As you can imagine, this was not easy without serious conversation.

However, I did accompany one of them in a taxi taking him to a hospital appointment. He said that exclusive communion with one's God, as one's closest friend, was the greatest privilege that any human being could have, and the source of a happiness that no one else could imagine or experience.

I had, and have, not the slightest reason to doubt that he was telling me the truth, since what he said has been said by many holy people for many centuries, people who came to be seen as saints.

Once I was visiting Delhi. In Old Delhi, the masses of human beings walk quickly, crammed together, somehow managing to find their own way through the mass. An occasional rickshaw or even a car manages to weave its own way through. I was staying at a crazily opulent hotel in New Delhi, gleaming marble from floor to ceiling, people leading the very non-simple life, expensively, and probably miserably.

Going for a walk one day, I came across an old man sitting on the kerb of a road. I stopped and smiled at him. He smiled back with what I can only call a seraphic smile. Not a word I often use. White teeth, lively eyes. He was not begging. He wasn't even collecting plastic bottles, to make a rupee or two.

He possessed nothing, literally nothing, in this world. He seemed to need nothing. His life was a simple as a human life can possibly be. And he seemed to me to be as deeply happy as any human being could be.

In a café in Venice, I spoke to a man called Pierluigi, who turned out to be a free-lance sailor, descendant of countless generations of Sicilian sailors. Red bandanna around his head. Weather-beaten face and arms.

A sailor's distant look in the eyes, which comes from staring into the far distance across the oceans of the world. He told me that he simply takes his boat and goes wherever he feels like going, taking a temporary job here and there, to finance the basics.

With my own non-simple life, I admit I felt a pathetic pang of envy. I asked him to get in touch, if ever his exercise of the freedom of the high seas should bring him to the port of London.

As you can understand, these experiences, and others like them, have haunted me, and they have led me improbably into fairly serious philosophy.

People wearing any kind of official uniform surrender their life to those whom they serve. We assume that they retain some sort of inner life. Hegel made a philosophy out of the idea that the self is determined by the other. Marx made a philosophy out of the idea that the self is made by society, including even our consciousness.

Sartre made a philosophy out of the case of the waiter, playing perfectly the part of being a waiter in a cafe. Each of us exists only as the performer of the role imposed on us by others. Wittgenstein made a philosophy out of the idea that we are what we say, and what we say means playing by the rules of various games we didn't invent.

Foucault made a philosophy out of the way that society classes some people as mad or criminal, and takes absolute power over them as such, as it does over those whom it classes as worker, consumer, rich, poor, powerful, powerless, or whatever.

We admire the eccentric, the martyr, the Leonardo of creativity, defiantly living the life of a self-determining human being. In the modern world of total socialising, few, if any of us, can even have the ambition to lead the life of the self-determining human being. Alienated, from the Latin word *alienus*, belonging to someone else. The alienated life of the modern world is, in one sense, a simpler life. It is certainly not a simple life.

'I don't think you're cut out for the simple life, Philip,' Mollie said, when I was visiting her some months later. 'You're too set in your ways. You don't lead an indulgent life, but you must have your own modest luxuries. Stick to the gardening. The purest of pleasures, if not the simplest.'

Mollie Maine playing the improbable part of the Turkish wise man, advising me, an improbable Candide.

She herself seemed like a new person now, free of unwanted cares and commitments and demands on her time. Plenty of gardening, of course. A down-sized life, a more self-determined life, if not exactly a simple life.

And what about me? You, dear reader, are wondering. I retire next year. I have decided to use my retirement lump sum to help to buy a house and a bit of land near a place called Èze, in the hills above Nice in southern France.

Passionate gardener, proud enough of my English garden, permanently frustrated by its northern micro-climate, living the perennial ecstasy of English gardeners sensually assaulted by the impossible panoply of a southern European garden at its most extreme.

Jacaranda and jasmine, fuchsia and hibiscus and melissa and hortensia, clematis and calendula and genista. Pelargoniums in every form. Torrents of bougainvillea. Lakes of lavender. Roses and roses and roses.

I will totally ignore the worldly temptations of Nice and Cannes. I will lead a vegetatively luxuriant, not a luxurious, life. A down-sized life, a more self-determined life, if not exactly the simple life. Dedicated to the purest of pleasures. And, who knows, I might even find myself getting closer to the First Gardener, without the need for Cistercian strictures or absolute spiritual purity.

MORAL
To live a simple life requires a lot of effort,
and enough money.

* * *

Twenty-Four

LOST TIME REGAINED

THE FUTURE OF THE PAST
Brave world that has such people in it

'Time past is part of time present,' Don Quixote said. 'I still weep when I think of the death of my lovely Rocinante,' he said. 'I had made him what he was. And some of me died with him.'

Don Quixote was the perfect host. Dispensing Manchego cheese and *Ibérico* ham and black olives and Garnacha wine, and other indigenous Spanish delicacies, plus his own wit and wisdom.

We have met all his guests before, each in their own familiar setting.

'It's not difficult to love a horse,' Gertrude Stein said. 'They're nicer than most human beings.'

She, sans Toklas and sans Oedipus, would say that the other guests were not the sort of people one would consort with in normal circumstances.

'I invested in horses at one time,' Denis Dobson said, a thinking businessman who nearly changed the world. 'Thoroughbreds, you understand. An efficient way to get rid of money fast, but a nice way.'

'I once rode in the Kentucky Derby,' Harry French, licensed charmer, said. 'Well, almost. I had got close to a notorious breeder-owner, professionally as it were, and he let me ride out his horse, the day before the wretched creature ran in the race, came in third, and was promptly disqualified for doping.'

'I had the occasional flutter on the horses,' Maggie Blyth, a special woman, said. 'I had an uncle who'd been a jockey. He taught me to know about sires and dams, and current form, and the Racing Post. I can't say it helped me all that much, moneywise. But it made it more interesting to watch the races.'

'I take it you didn't think to use probability theory, madam.' J.S. Bunyan, rogue philosopher, said, managing, as usual, to convey disdain for both the interlocutor and the topic. Why are philosophers so competitive, even with people who are not their competitors? Some sort of insecurity, perhaps.

'Not exactly, no,' Maggie said.

'You would have known that the improbability of a particular horse winning a particular race is infinity-minus-one. And you would have saved your money.'

'But it would have been less fun. Did you never bet on horses, Professor?'

'Of course, I do. But randomly. And I sometimes win.'

'We used to wonder whether it's blasphemous to pray to God for help in picking a winner,' Sister Monica, a happy nun, said. 'Hard to resist, given His infinite wisdom. I remember a Mass in Ireland where the bidding prayers included a prayer for the local team to win the Gaelic Football Championship.'

'Did they win, dear lady?'

'No. Which made me more scrupulous in the matter.'

'We are all the product of chance,' Mollie Maine, the ultimate gardener, said. 'A seed is sown. It may be in dry ground or rocky ground or in clay, as the good book says. And we are born to flourish, or else to just get by.'

'I didn't realise gardening was a philosophical thing,' Serena Stangle, re-born intellectual, said.

'Nothing more so,' Mollie said. 'You learn your place in the universe, between God and

Nature. The ultimate humility. Without evil. Gardeners are usually nicer people. Like the best sort of religious people.'

'It's strange,' Serena said. 'However much education we get, we never seem to learn what exactly is our place in the universe. We're like lost sheep.'

'We are what we are,' J.S. Bunyan said, 'And that's an end on't.'

'For heaven's sake,' Edgar Sibling, self-making chancer, said. 'It's not the end on't. We have plans and purposes. We make things happen. Sometimes we make things better. I reject group thinking, one-dimensional thinking, cliché thinking. I am my own person. I am alone. I am at one with everyone else who feels alone. I have the privilege of being young. Life is what you make of it. With a lot of luck and a lot of effort and a lot of help.'

'You're right, Edgar,' Cardinal Castelfranco, wise old priest, said. 'And I have the other privilege, of being old. We are moral beings. We judge. We choose. We take responsibility. Individually and collectively. It's quite a burden.'

'Thinking about everything is the privilege of the human species,' Manu Narayan, Indian wise man, said. 'Our gift from evolution or from the order of the universe. An ambiguous gift. Another burden. It means we make our own world. And have to live in it. No excuses. No escape.'

'I've spent most of my life at the collective end of things,' Harry French said, 'Diplomacy involves a lot of judging and a lot of choosing. Sadly, most of it is bad judging and bad choosing. Governments are like dim human beings when they're not simply crooks. You've got to make allowances for them. But the strange thing is, sometimes things do get better. God only knows how.'

'Nothing is but thinking makes it so. If I may quote a close relative of mine, a Prince of Denmark, no less.'

Don Quixote certainly caught the attention of the party.

'If people stopped thinking,' he persisted, 'everything would be goodness and sweetness and light, faster than you can say Jack Robinson, as the English say. Mark my words.'

'You're right, Monsieur Quixote,' Marie-Hélène Biron said. She is that French invention, namely, the professional intellectual, who was able to escape from that fate by way of love. 'We in France worship rationality, and, somehow at the same time, we don't trust its products. Rationality produces more irrationality in the world than you could shake a stick at, as the English also rather mysteriously say. Rationality has never been a failing of the English.'

'We English muddle through,' Thomas Grange said, aristocrat taken from his past. 'Been doing it for centuries. I am the living embodiment of the muddle of my ancestors, some of them not entirely right in their heads. It agitates the French, how we get away with it. But a passive view of life does lead to big downs as well as big ups, I must admit.'

'The English and the Americans escape into fantasies of themselves and their past,' Manu Narayan said. 'Alternative realities that make things easier to live with. Causes problems when they have to meet some awful real reality from time to time.'

'Science and technology have changed everything,' Gavin Meredith, tech wizard, said. 'They are the reality that excludes fantasy. The danger is that they may exclude all other forms of thought, the forms which should govern our lives, and which should put science and technology in their proper place.'

'Why don't privileged people admit their

own privilege?' Maggie Blyth said. 'They can't imagine what it's like to be born at a disadvantage, and to have to make your own life despite all your disadvantages.'

'I was born privileged, I suppose,' Joe Giorgione, who had suddenly grown older in Manhattan, said. 'But you can see beyond your privilege. Just live for a while in New York. All human life is there. In all its terrible inequality. You can try to look the other way, but it haunts you for ever.'

'I was in prison for a crime I didn't commit,' Bill Sykes, victim of justice, said. 'But, for all that time, I was as close as it's possible to be to the cruel and crude effects of social disadvantage and social inequality. It changed me for ever. Joe says that you try to put such things out of your mind. I can't.'

'I came to doubt what I'd spent my life on,' John Doe said, the banker whom we met getting lost, in more ways than one. 'Making money out of money. We take over people's hard-won hard-working businesses, putting people out of work to make the business more profitable, until we can sell it off at a hefty profit, and move on to something else. Devouring widows' houses, the Bible calls it.'

'Compound interest is magic,' Gertrude Stein said, 'Alchemy, turning lumps of money into oceans of money, without the slightest bit of effort.'

'Money makes the world go round,' Ernie Wilde said, English man among English men. 'Greed is the root of all evil, as the Bible also said. But where would capitalism be without it? We should bless you and your kind, John, for being public benefactors. As Adam Smith or someone said, private vice added together makes public benefit. Speeding offences support the local economy. Think of bees in the beehive. Or ants in the ant-hill.'

'There's a high price to pay for bee-like collectivism,' Greta May, defiant aesthete, said. 'Cultural events are supported by rich people, rarely for the best of reasons, usually for unworthy reasons. Meanwhile, society becomes more or more uncultured, more and more undereducated, in a state of all-consuming laziness, shunning anything difficult. The highest achievements of the human imagination become exotic, like cricket or croquet. The preserve of the peculiar few.'

'I wouldn't disparage cricket,' J.S. Bunyan said. 'Cricket and football made the British

Empire. They unite people across the world to this day. They have beautiful cricket pitches in Abu Dhabi.'

'People should study Britain as a unique form of civilisation,' Jack Gaddi, American Anglophile, said. 'Very hard to make sense of it. But it has survived, unlike the Roman Empire. Britain lives on in its progeny all over the world.'

'Rome lived on in the Holy Roman Church,' Don Quixote said. 'I remember it well.'

'And when the Roman Church was pushed into the side-lines in Europe,' Dorothea Dorn, young historian, said, 'nationalism and moral confusion replaced it.'

'In France, we worry that high culture and high cuisine are fading away,' Mme Biron said. 'They were the hall-mark of French civilisation. We civilised Europe and an empire. Nobody seems to care about such things nowadays.'

'I've always lived in the past,' Don Quixote said. 'My past was a better place, a place of chivalry and courtly love and faith in God.'

'I am trying to live in the future,' Gavin Meredith said. 'The past is beyond redemption. The future is our only hope.'

'I agree with Edgar.' David Barclay, accidental hero, said. 'I too am a self-determining person.

Inner-directed. A private income helps, I admit. And being young. But I think you're all being too pessimistic. What is new is that everything that used to be available only to a tiny minority in society is now available to everyone. The past is a smorgasbord, a buffet full of delights, for us to pick and choose in making our present and our future.'

'The Internet contains everything human beings have ever achieved,' Ernie Wilde said. 'And there it is for us, at the click of a button, free of charge. To make of it what we can.'

'The Google Enlightenment,' Gertrude Stein said. 'Information masquerading as knowledge.'

'The human mind is withering way,' Steve Ruskin, people-watcher, said. 'And soon it will be unable to know what being human used to be.'

'I must say I've recently become rather interested in religion,' J.S. Bunyan said. 'Voltaire and natural science were supposed to put an end to it.

'But it goes on. Some of it much improved. Some of it worse than ever. But I do wonder if the human race can survive without religion, in some shape or form.'

'I'll tell you something I discovered recently,' Edgar Sibling said. 'Many of the famous nineteenth-century doubters of religion were the sons of German Lutheran pastors. Even Dostoevsky had a father problem. In some Freudianish way, this made them into closet seekers after religion. What if God really is dead? Will we survive? They agonised over those questions to the edge of insanity.'

'It seems to me' Cardinal Castelfranco said, 'that the present chaotic state of the world is making many people feel a spiritual void in their lives, the lack of a transcendental dimension.'

'Some of us never lost it,' Manu Narayan said.

'Pining for the forbidden fruit that they themselves have forbidden,' J.B. Bunyan said.

'Aren't we all?' Serena Stangle said.

'As I see it,' Sister Monica said, 'religion is not about believing a list of things put into words. It's a way of living your life, struggling to be good, and to do good, to avoid doing evil. And the Church is there to help us to do that, and to bring people together to share the struggle.'

'I'm certainly not religious,' Gavin Meredith said, 'but I've come to believe that there is a way we could restore the higher dimension of human life. It begins with imagining the ideal human being, and then re-engineering human society with that ideal as its master plan. Applied idealism. True humanism.'

'Time past is present in time future.' Don Quixote said. 'All being is becoming. The human species will survive if human beings remember what being human could be.'

We will leave their discussion at that point. The author takes some pride in having caused all these people to share something of their lives, in most cases at a time of transition in their personal entelechies, all of them faced by a human future more uncertain than ever. They come from only one small part of the human race. They may or may not be more widely representative.

The reader may wonder about one or two people who were not present at the after-party, our own modest Proustian *bal des têtes*.

Mrs Glampworthy, aka Lady Eliza Tolpuddle, whose soufflés failed to souffle, has taken holy orders. She is parish priest of a combined parish in Gloucestershire. She also manages the local Meals on Wheels service. She says she has no episcopal ambitions.

Septimus Maximus Blenkinsop, solicitor, and his wife Magnolia, have retired to Delray

Beach, Florida. He is a co-owner of Shady Pines Golf Club and Hotel. She is the owner of the Lost Loves Funeral Home. An each-way bet, given the demography of Florida.

Matthew Broad, troubled historian, is still optimistic about a New Enlightenment in the twenty-first century. But he is hedging his bet on the human future by doing up a house on the Atlantic coast of Ireland, where he can be alone with the power of Nature under the power of God, in a place with an interesting past and a calming present. He is still close to Manu Narayan who persists in seeing our troubled times in the perspective of an ancient culture that has experienced everything.

Frank Price, the English man with doubts about the meaning of life, has joined an amateur choir. He finds that singing sacred music is consoling.

Dorothea Dorn, who was present at the Lost Time party, has published her thesis under the title *Churches and States. The End of Christendom in Europe*. For a while, she saw her future in the financial world, where you are appropriately rewarded for having an active mind, rather than the academy, where you aren't. But she has taken up a post at the University of Kiel.

We should also mention that David Barclay, who was also a guest at the Lost Time party, divides his time between his apartment in Albany, London, and the lower floors of Cardinal Castelfranco's house on the Grand Canal in Venice, which he purchased on remarkably reasonable terms.

There is one other person whose tale might have been told here, but whose accumulation of despair was too great to share. Despair at the enormity of human evil, our constant failure to do what we know to be good. Despair at the condition of the planet Earth, the human world, the human species, human society, the human being, and the human mind. What the human species, made by God or by Nature, has made of itself. Despair at the human future.

But humankind cannot bear that much reality. We must all get on with the job of living everyday life as best we can and despite everything.

What are the moral lessons that we might have learned from sharing significant moments in the lives of the people whose tales are told here?

Our lives are an evolutionary process, adapting ourselves to our changing circumstances. Engage with the wonder of Now, the kairos, *the ever-new moment with its unlimited possibilities, which can change our life, our personal* metanoia. *Seek the best. Think for yourself. Don't be deceived by appearances. Share your inner life with others. Keep hoping, despite everything. Top up the engine from time to time with a bit of* joie de vivre.

Lessons that we should already have learned from the many enlightenments of the human mind over the course of the last thirty centuries.

* * *

EPILOGUE
Breaking news

Dorothea Dorn and Harry French are engaged to be married. He is now at the British embassy in Vienna.

Marie-Hélène Biron and Yves-Matthieu have been blessed with a daughter, Héloïse.

Serena Stangle and Bill Sykes are working together on prison reform.

Maggie Blyth and Jack Gaddi have met several times. He is helping her with her writing. A transatlantic special relationship in the making?

The participants in the Lost Time party have agreed to meet again in two years' time, if the human species still exists then.

And me? I will soon be cultivating my paradise garden at Èze when I finally placate the whims and vagaries of post-Brexit French bureaucracy. No heaven without a bit of purgatory. Mollie Maine has promised to be my first visitor.